REUNION IN NORWAY

Dec 29, 2003
Phoenix, AZ

To Brody

and Joan

REUNION IN NORWAY

JONATHAN MARSHALL

old friends are

Best Jon

RUDER FINN PRESS

Editorial Director: Susan Slack
Creative Director: Emily Korsmo
Design: Ruder Finn Design, New York

First published in the United States in 2004 by
Ruder Finn Press, Inc.
301 East 57th Street
New York, NY 10022

ISBN #: 0-9720119-9-4

Printed in the United States of America

This book is dedicated to my wife, Maxine Marshall,
who shared our adventure in Norway with me
and encouraged me to write this book.

contents

acknowledgements

To my wife, Maxine Marshall, for excellent criticism of the various drafts of this book.

To my assistant and secretary, Jan Laurant, who kept my computer working and helped in dozens of ways.

To Wendy Ring, for perceptive editing and criticism.

To my old friend, David Finn, for having the confidence to undertake this publication.

To Sarah Harrell, for editing help during the early stages of writing.

To Dr. Ron Carlson of Arizona State University's Creative Writing department, for expert criticism and encouragement.

To Professor Steve Batalden, for providing background information about Norway.

And to the men of the Theta Group in Bergen who inspired this story — the story of their heroic work during World War II.

In 1992 my wife, Maxine, and I traveled to Scandinavia. In Copenhagen and Oslo we visited elaborate museums that chronicled the events in Denmark and Norway during World War II. The messages were powerful and they made the war years come alive in our minds.

Later we visited Bergen, a beautiful city on the west coast of Norway. It's surrounded by seven mountains and has a large and vibrant harbor. While in Bergen we had dinner at an excellent restaurant located on the second floor of a building that in medieval times had been the headquarters for the local Hanseatic League, a trading group of mercantile towns. We learned that the building also housed a small World War II museum on the third floor. We climbed the stairs and discovered a small room that had been restored to show how the Norwegian underground had operated a radio service from Bergen to inform the Norwegian government in exile and the British of German naval activity in the area.

The room had been hidden in a storage area and contained two beds, a table and chairs, as well as radio equipment. A friendly docent told us that the underground members called themselves the Theta group. She explained their activities and gave us a small booklet that told the Theta story. The group was part of a network of resistance fighters, many of them fishermen, who operated a shuttle of supplies and personnel aboard fishing boats that traveled to and from the western coast of Norway and the Shetland Islands, an operation known as the Shetland Bus.

Upon returning home, I kept thinking about Bergen and the Theta group, whose important and brave war efforts are hardly known outside of Norway. The idea for *Reunion in Norway* soon began to take shape. All of the characters are fictional, as is the story, but the activities of the underground organization—The Fishermen—featured in the book are based on the work of the Theta patriots.

— Jonathan Marshall

chapter one

NOVEMBER 1941

A SHOCK OF curly red hair tumbled out from under a gray stocking cap. Ollie Larsen saw a pair of deep blue eyes above ruddy cheeks look down from the gunwale of the rocking fishing boat, illuminated with small red, yellow, and white running lights on the hull and masts. Then a pair of huge shoulders rose above the vessel's side.

[handwritten margin note: ? yellow should be green]

"*Velkommen, velkommen.* My name is Erik the Red," the giant shouted in Norwegian. "I hope you like fishing in Norway," he said in a deep voice that boomed over the noise of the waves, the screaming wind, and the motors of the fishing boat and the small British launch that carried Ollie.

The agents on either side of Ollie raised their pistols at the red-haired man.

They had already endured a long journey, racing north and east from the special operations base in northern Scotland to this meeting. It had been a frightening ride, bouncing through the roughest seas Ollie had ever experienced. For more than seven hours the three-man crew had navigated roughly one hundred miles through heavy waves and freezing rain, escaping German detection by sheer luck and speed. And now at last they had met

[handwritten margin note: cruising at 14 knots]

their Norwegian contact to deliver the launch's cargo—Sergeant Oliver Larsen, along with his radio supplies and high powered explosives hidden in three wooden barrels marked "FISKEN," Norwegian for "fish."

It was well past two on a blustery, dark winter afternoon. The British boat bobbed up and down, threatening to toss Ollie and the others into the angry black water. The excitement and tension of traveling through the North Sea, which was patrolled by the Germans, both by air and water, had occupied Ollie's complete attention. And now, with the two boats finally rendezvousing, he became aware that his face felt painfully frozen from the cold salt spray and strong wind as he tried to tell the fisherman his own code words. "I am Olaf the Viking," Ollie yelled in Norwegian. "I come to send fish to market."

Although they had both given the proper verbal identifications, Ollie was still nervous, wary of a possible trap, because the redheaded Norwegian didn't immediately toss him a rope, the final signal. Instead Erik stood to his full height. He was enormous, the biggest man Ollie had ever seen, surely seven feet tall. He said, "Skynd seg," telling Ollie to hurry up.

Hurry up for what, Ollie thought. He wasn't going to rush to his own execution. Instead, he arced his index finger around the trigger of the Thompson sub-machine gun that he held concealed under his rain poncho.

Then a broad grin spread across Erik's ruddy face. "Sorry," he said in Norwegian, before flicking the British crew a line.

"It's good," Ollie told his men before one of the agents holstered his gun and tied the rope fast, pulling the two boats closer. Erik threw a rope ladder over the side.

Ollie found himself smiling back at Erik even though with his frozen lips it felt more like a grimace. Only now, however, did Ollie release the trigger on the gun, which he then handed to one of the British sailors before he slung his duffel over his back. Then Ollie climbed up and aboard the fishing boat.

Standing on the deck behind Erik was a young, blond man wearing a blue cap with a rifle in his hands, the barrel pointed at Ollie, who raised his arms. Erik looked at Ollie, then turned around. "OK," Erik told the other man, who nodded his head before stashing the rifle under a tarpaulin at his feet, near one of the masts. "That's Sven. He's a good fisherman and a crack rifle shot," he said in Norwegian to Ollie.

"I'm glad he didn't take a crack at me," Ollie said as Erik motioned for the man to join them at the gunwale. Sven was tall, over six feet, but he looked almost slight next to the giant Erik.

Like a bucket brigade, the British agents passed over the two barrels of radio equipment to Ollie, Erik, and Sven. Last was the barrel of explosives. "Light touch with that 'til you use it on the Nazis," one said to Ollie.

"Godspeed," said another before the rope was untied and thrown back to the fishing boat. Then the British launch turned and motored away.

Sven stood beside Ollie and held his hand out while staring at the deck. His fingers were small and red with cold but his grip was crushing, as though he wanted to prove how tough he was.

"*God mote De*," Ollie told Sven, who continued to stare at the deck.

"He doesn't talk much, but he's glad to make your acquaintance," Erik said, then directed Sven to carry the barrels down to the cabin. Sven picked up Ollie's duffel first and walked away, weaving as he did from the waves and the wind.

"I need to relieve Evold in the wheelhouse," Erik told Ollie. "He's been there almost four hours while we circled waiting to pick you up, trying not to attract attention. We've seen a few of their planes." He scowled at Ollie, as if he'd been personally responsible for the delay.

"We lost time while evading their patrols, and the weather," Ollie said.

"Speaking of evading, let me see your papers," Erik said. "They've been targeting the fishing boats. They know that some of us are part of the underground. So if one of their patrol boats stops us, your papers must be in order."

Ollie handed him the counterfeit identification papers. Erik studied them carefully. "They are good, very good," he nodded at last. Then he rubbed the papers against his wet pants and handed them back to Ollie. "So they don't look new," Erik said, before walking to the wheelhouse. Ollie followed.

Erik took the wheel from another tall man, though this one was thinner than Erik and Sven. He had black hair that was dark and shiny as a pair of dress shoes. "Olaf, this is Evold," Erik said.

"We meet finally," Evold said as Ollie shook his hand.

"Go eat. Warm up, my friend," Erik told Evold.

"For a spell," Evold said before leaving.

The boat lifted up and down in the heavy swells. Ollie wanted to follow Evold below, away from the wet sea spray and the cold wind. Even though he had trained for this assignment off Scotland in small boats, his stomach churned from the long journey and his general discomfort from being on the water.

Just then a small man came up on the bridge. "Your face tells me that you are not a sailor," he said in a deep voice, looking hard at Ollie. "So if you are sick, do not throw up to windward or it will blow back into the boat."

"I'll try to remember that," Ollie said.

"Our friend will be all right, Ake," Erik said to the short, black-bearded man, who was only about five foot three in height but strong and stocky, as if he were five foot three in width, too. He had broad shoulders and large calloused hands. His smile showed a gold tooth. Ollie thought he looked like an ancient Norwegian troll. Erik said, "Ollie will get his sea legs soon. But now it is time to look like a real fisherman's boat. You and Sven set the net." Then Erik slowed the boat.

From the bridge, Ollie watched the two men work together to release the heavy net off the stern and into the sea.

"We must fill the hold so if the Germans stop us they will not suspect that we have been doing anything other than fishing," Erik said. "Besides, they don't like to be near the fish. Too smelly for them. The trick will come later, when we take your equipment away from the harbor. It will go with the fish to Eduard, a wholesaler who is our friend. He will repackage everything into canned food cases and we will bring it to our hideout where you can begin your work."

"I don't know much about your operation, or Bergen, Erik. I was supposed to be sent to Trondheim," Ollie said. "But things went wrong there. A bridge was dynamited and the Gestapo sent agents in to comb the town, house to house, trying to locate the underground. It was too dangerous to send a new man in for a while. Then the man who was supposed to come to Bergen broke his ankle during a training run, so they changed my assignment a day before I was to leave. Plans had already been made to meet you and I was trained and available. But there was no time for a thorough briefing." Ollie held his hands aloft as though he was praying. Then he shrugged and laughed. "That's the military for you," he said to Erik who alternated looking intently at his face and concentrating on the sea ahead.

"Unpredictable, much like fishing," Erik said.

"So tell me everything you can—your operation, your people, the town," Ollie said, spreading his legs to steady himself and fight the motion of the boat. "How many are you and who are you?"

Erik peered into the murky light of the late afternoon winter sky before answering. "There's twenty-five of us, although some only do special jobs when needed. And then we have friends. They don't know where our hide-outs are. The fewer the better, you know. We call ourselves The Fishermen," he said. "We've known each other since we were small boys, we know what each can do, and we trust each other entirely." He paused and looked at the compass and then up at the flag. The stiffening wind had shifted and Ollie saw that the clouds were growing thicker. A light rain began to fall. Ollie crossed his arms, pulling his poncho tighter around him.

"I think we're in for a bit of a blow tonight, but our boat is sturdy and our crew is experienced, so do not worry, Olaf. In fact, a little storm is good because the Germans will keep in the harbors. They are not good sailors like Norwegians and they don't like heavy weather."

"The Fishermen formed after the Germans demanded that our king surrender our country. But the king and our prime minister refused to be puppets for the Nazis. We decided to fight for our country once our king, his family, and a few top government officials escaped to England where they set up our government in exile," Erik said. He turned to look directly at Ollie and raised his voice almost to a shout to be heard over the pelting rain and gusting wind. "Why doesn't America join the war and help us fight?"

Ollie opened his mouth to speak but he wasn't sure what to say. He couldn't easily explain his nation's neutrality. He hadn't been as reticent. He had volunteered with the Canadians to fight the Germans in 1940 for a very personal and private reason. The year before, Ollie's maternal grandmother, who long before had immigrated to America from Bavaria, received a smuggled note from an old friend who reported that two of his grand-mother's sisters and their families had been taken away with other Jews from their village to Nazi labor camps. Ollie's grandmother had been unable to find out where her relatives were and if they were even still alive. Ollie had been raised Lutheran and grew up on flat ground in the middle of the country, but suddenly this war far across the ocean on foreign lands, in the countries of his ancestors, was his. He felt that someone in his family had to fight back for the family members who couldn't. And since he was the only member of the Larsen family who was of fighting age, he enlisted.

If it had been up to Ollie, the United States would have joined the war along with the British and French. But he told Erik, "Our political situation is complicated and our Constitution requires that our president get an agreement from Congress to declare war. President Roosevelt can't just decide on his own. We're slow sometimes, but once we get in we'll give them a hell of a fight. Like we did in the first war."

Erik held tight to the wheel, struggling to keep the boat on course. Meanwhile, Ollie shivered with cold, his teeth chattering.

"How are you organized?" Ollie asked, stamping his feet to try to warm himself.

"We divided The Fishermen into two groups, split between the city and the harbor," Erik continued. "We found safe houses to store guns, food, and equipment. And then everything happened faster than expected. The Germans struck so quickly and with so much power that our army could not fight them off. They marched into every city, dropped bombs, took prisoners. They fly the swastika over our towns."

Ollie stared into the overcast horizon and Erik's sudden silence.

"I think there's something ahead," Erik said, picking up a pair of binoculars hanging on a nail and studying the shrouded distance.

Ollie stood in the small wheelhouse peering into the wind-driven spray, trying to see what had alerted Erik. He saw only the dark water, occasionally lined with white foam.

"Go below and tell Evold to come up right away," Erik told him.

Ollie, stiff with cold and immobility, climbed down a steep ladder into the cabin below that smelled of fish, salt, and tobacco. There was a bunk on each side and at the far end stood a small stove and food locker. At the foot of the gangway there were wooden pegs on which to hang wet heavy clothing and below were Ollie's duffel and the barrels. The space was warm and dim, lit by a kerosene lamp on a small table at which sat Evold and another man with a large nose and broad shoulders.

"Erik needs you in the wheelhouse," Ollie said to Evold, who slipped on the suspenders of his bib overalls, put on his jacket, and pulled on a pair of rubber boots. Then he hurried up to the deck with Ollie close behind him.

When they reached the wheelhouse Erik stepped aside and handed Evold the binoculars. "What do you make of her?" he asked.

Evold studied a far away shape. Now Ollie could just see the gray outline of a large ship in the distance, seemingly heading toward their boat.

"It doesn't look like a patrol, or a warship," Evold said quietly. "Looks more like a merchantman. But it could be German. Think we're on a collision course?"

"We can't take a chance and give them an opportunity to ram us, Evold," Erik said. "There'd be no rescue and the water's damned cold, which is a hell of a way to go. Should we give way?"

"We have the lights on and the net is out. Nothing suspicious in that," Evold said. "If it's the Huns we want them to think we're not hiding. Let's stay the course."

Erik turned to Ollie and said, "We have extra power built into the engine, but not enough to run from their patrol boats, which are very fast, so we must out-think them."

As Ollie watched the other ship, he thought in his mind, "Turn, turn, turn," wishing he could will the vessel away, but it continued to approach the fishing boat. In his first assignment with the Royal Canadian Air Force, Ollie had manned a radio in a bomber. While on bombing runs, he was used to feeling as though he and the pilot were the hunters. Now he felt as though he was the one being hunted. During training for this assignment, Ollie had heard stories about other Norwegian fishing boats carrying agents and supplies that were captured en route to or from the Shetland Islands, where the Norwegian resistance movement was based. He knew the consequence for what the Nazis called "Feindbegungsstingung." Being caught aiding the enemy ended with a bullet to the head, but not before those accused were tortured to extract information about the underground's operations.

"Looks like she's charting a different course," Evold finally said as the larger ship began to move starboard. Soon it became apparent that the other boat had no interest in intercepting the fishing boat. The vessel grew smaller in the distance.

Ollie leaned back against a railing, relieved.

As he watched the other ship sail away, his mind went back to the time he first learned of this assignment and Royal Canadian Air Force Sergeant Ollie

Larsen, an American, was ushered into a shabby green Quonset hut at the English military base in Leuchars, northern Scotland. The sole sign on the door identified it as the Norske Education Office, harmless sounding. He had not known why he had been told to report there.

The walls of the small office were covered with maps of Norway and the room smelled of stale cigarette smoke. Ollie came to a quick salute before a tall, thin British major with a bushy gray mustache.

The man had a thin face with a prominent jaw and steel-gray eyes. He stood ramrod straight in a perfectly pressed khaki uniform. He wore no decorations, although one picture on the wall to the side showed him receiving a medal. The major focused narrow squinting eyes on him.

Ollie knew this was a tough no-nonsense officer. His nametag said Oglesby, his only identification.

Probebly would not have that nametag.

"At ease, Sergeant. Have a seat," he ordered in a deep voice as he extended his hand.

"Larsen, Ollie, Royal Canadian Air Force, radio expert, wanted to be a pilot but couldn't make landings. Trained as a radio expert and navigator instead." The major read from a file on an otherwise clean desktop. He stopped and smiled. "I had the same problem, son. Cracked up two bloody training planes, so now I'm in charge of a special training program instead of being on the front line."

Oglesby continued to look at him and said, "Single. Two years of college. Joined the RCAF in 1940. High marks on all tests. High school ski and track teams. Tough but idealistic. Anything else I should know, Larsen?"

"No, sir, but it was baseball and not track. Excuse me, sir, but what's this all about?"

"Weren't you told anything before coming here, son?" the major asked, frowning. "Bloody damn idiots, those RCAF desk officers."

The office was over-heated and Ollie felt uncomfortable. He wanted to squirm in his seat, but was not about to show any weakness, so he stared at the maps on the wall after a quick look at the major's neat desk with Ollie's file and one photograph.

"Yes, sir," Ollie replied with a straight face.

"Well, sergeant, it's like this. We have a bloody damn war and if you volunteer you just might be a hero. And you won't have to worry about anti-aircraft fire and getting shot down. You'll see a beautiful country and meet some brave, good people. It could be the greatest time of your life."

The man sounded like a travel agent pitching a resort, Ollie thought, but he realized the major was deadly serious. He was not playing a game or trying to be funny.

"Yes, sir," Ollie said, "and if I read you right I could get myself killed because whatever it is will be mighty dangerous. Am I right, sir?"

"Well, old boy, you could get killed, but everyone can get killed in a bloody war. That's the risk we take to preserve freedom. We fight like lions or the damn Nazis destroy us." He sounded as if he had memorized the answer before the question was asked.

"The Nazis could drop a bomb on this shitty hut this minute, or you could plant your boot on a mine." He stared at Ollie for a minute. "You mean seriously, Sergeant, that no one told you what the damned hell we are doing up here and why we wanted to talk with you? I say, that's a bad scene, so we might as well get it right from the start, Larsen. Pour yourself some coffee and listen."

Ollie got a cup of scalding hot black coffee, taking his time so that he could digest what was happening. He was not sure whether to be flattered or scared or excited. After he sat back down in the uncomfortable straight wooden chair, he studied Oglesby. Despite a slightly hesitant speech and upper crust British accent, Ollie could see a steel hardness in the thin intelligent face. The smile wrinkles around the major's mouth and the steady clear eyes seemed to indicate a man of both compassion and dedication. Another photograph showed the major carrying a very large pack and a heavy submachine gun, while a third showed him stripped to the waist leading a column of men in a desert somewhere.

In any event, the man seemed to know what he was doing and he commanded Ollie's respect.

"Well, the business starts in London," Oglesby said. "Mr. Churchill and the war cabinet are considering landings in Norway, or even a full-scale invasion to divert the Germans from France, possibly from the attack on Britain itself. I don't have to tell you that the war's going badly, damned badly. One bloody defeat after another." He said it angrily. "The war cabinet wants to take the pressure off and raise morale with a counter-attack. They also want to stop the Krauts from attacking ships from the States that are taking supplies to the Russkies up at Murmansk. They're taking a terrible toll sinking dozens of freighters and war ships every month. They're murdering our sailors," he added bitterly. "They torpedo the ships, and then they take target practice on the lifeboats and men clinging to life rafts. What a fuckin' sick way to fight a war."

He paused, opened another pack of cigarettes. "Smoke, Larsen?"

Ollie declined and sipped his coffee.

The major blew smoke out of the corner of his mouth. "We have friends in Norway. In fact, there's a growing underground up there, but outside of Oslo, it's mostly isolated, untrained people in small towns. In Trondheim, Trømso, Bergen, other small cities. In order for them to be effective, to feed us information, they have to be able to communicate. The only way this can be done is by radio. Am I right, Sergeant?"

It took Ollie a brief moment to realize what the major was leading up to. He sat forward slightly so he could judge what this cool officer was saying.

"I guess so. Sounds logical. And you want me, a guy who mans a radio in a bomber, to run a radio in Norway and tell you where the hell the Germans are hiding? Sounds like exciting duty, Major." Ollie took a few careful sips of coffee to give him time to consider. "But I don't think I'm qualified."

"We'll be the judge of that, son. We're looking for forty young, strong, bright soldiers who know radios and explosives. They'll receive intense training and then be sent to different places in Norway and Denmark one at a time. You will be one of the first if you are chosen. We're also looking for men who have ancestors from Norway or still have family there. Yours come from Trømso, correct?"

"No, sir, my grandparents came to the States from Stavanger."

Ogelsby looked at Larsen's file again and frowned. "Doesn't matter, old chap. Bergen, Trømso, Trondheim, Stavanger, they're all the same. They're north and on the west coast, and they're cut off by the German fuckin' navy and the bloody secret police. Eventually we want to train several hundred Norwegians to track German ships, locate troop concentrations and sabotage their bridges, airfields and railroads. And, of course, we want our operators to feed us reliable information. So we need a radio network along the west coast.

"The Norwegians are jolly brave people, but they can't operate, or survive, in a vacuum. We have to get them the bloody equipment and train them." He stubbed out his cigarette and got himself another cup of coffee.

Ollie studied the maps on the wall, then rose restlessly. It sounded dangerous, and exciting. He wondered if he had the courage and stamina for the assignment. He waited tensely for more details.

Major Oglesby sat down again. "Now I have some questions for you, Larsen. First, why did you leave college and volunteer right after the Nazis marched into Poland? It wasn't your war and the damned French were still fighting. You're not even a Canadian. You're a Yank, at least that's what the record says, why?"

"I had my reasons, sir," Ollie replied. "I'd never been out of Minnesota and a small part of Canada, and the RCAF seemed like a good way to start seeing the world. My father ran a big grain elevator and I was a small town boy. So I wanted excitement, and I wanted to be with people who could see beyond the next wheat field. Also, I had broken up with my girlfriend and I wanted to maybe meet some new girls." He blushed slightly. "Well, I did meet some girls in various pubs, but pick-ups were not the kind of thing I wanted," he said with some embarrassment.

"And I didn't like college much. I wanted some excitement, I guess. I'd always been sort of a quiet outdoors guy, liked camping in the woods, didn't get myself in trouble." He smiled. "Here was a chance to, well, maybe fly a fighter plane and shoot down enemy planes. This was a chance to be a hero. It sounded good in theory, even if I didn't know what it would all be like. I never even thought about the possibility of danger, getting killed or flunking flight lessons."

He paused and grinned at the major. "What a laugh. I never could figure how close the plane was to the ground, so the flight instructors decided I'd wreck too many of our planes and they made me a radio operator and navigator instead. It was cheaper." *Repetition*

He watched as the smoke from another cigarette enveloped the major's face and curled into the already smoky room. "But there was one other thing, sir." He stopped and looked down at the floor for a moment.

"What was that, son?" Oglesby asked sharply.

It took Ollie a few seconds to reply. Then softly he said, "My one grandmother's Jewish. She grew up in Germany. A message was smuggled to her right after the war started in 1939. It said that her two sisters had been sent to a concentration camp near Munich. Three cousins had been murdered by the Nazis. All the close members of her family had been killed or sent to the camps. The message also said the Nazis were torturing Jews and others in the camps. She was devastated, obviously. The next time I saw her a few weeks later I could tell she had been crying. She looked years older. My grandmother had suddenly become an old lady. It hurt even more because she had told me a few years earlier that when I finished college she would take me to Bavaria where her family was. Now there will be no family." He took a deep breath, and finally was able to look up at the major again.

"I guess that's it, sir. Someone in our family had to fight back. Even though I'm not Jewish. I'm Lutheran. I want to get even and I'm the only one the right age." He thought for a moment then made a decision. "So what do you want me to do? Just don't give me a desk job, sir."

Ogelsby stared at the dossier on the desk in front of him, looked up at Larsen and then back at the dossier. He frowned and looked again at Ollie. At last in a cold voice he said, "None of our records show a German grandmother or a Jew. You're not making this up are you?" His tone was steely. "This assignment's too critical and we can't have any false information which might compromise it later. There's no place for liars in this operation. We'll hunt you down if you're a traitor," the major declared as he banged his fist down hard on his desk. "We kill traitors."

"Sir, it's all true."

"Bloody strange, bloody strange. How did they miss this?" He looked up and stared intensely at Ollie. "Who the hell are you, Sergeant?" he snapped. "What's your real bloody name? What's going on here?"

"My name is Sergeant Oliver Richard Larsen, but everyone calls me Ollie, and everything I've said is damn well true."

The major focused his gray eyes on Ollie's and glared. At last he spoke almost in a whisper. "OK Larsen, we'll check it. But if you're falsifying information you'll be subject to court martial. You understand? This is war. We hang traitors."

"Yes, sir, but everything I've said is true." Ollie banged his hand on the desk. Ogelsby stubbed out the cigarette, sat back in his chair and looked at him a long time. Ollie looked back, trying to remain calm. He realized his fists were clenched and he opened and closed his fingers to ease the tightness.

"Here's my question, Larsen. Do you want to keep riding bombers across the German shooting gallery, or do you want to go to Norway? You'll get damn little help and be largely on your own training radio operators in the underground. You'll go there alone. You'll work with Norwegian contacts, no Brits or Americans. You could get caught by the Gestapo. You know they don't play by the rules of civilized warfare, if there is such a thing." He paused and said even more softly, "I know what I'd choose."

Ollie was certain that Major Oglesby would opt for joining the Norwegian underground. There would be no hesitation. But Ollie wanted to stall for a few moments to think and he turned the question around. "Can I ask how you got this job, sir?" he asked.

"That's impertinent, Sergeant, but considering the assignment, it's fair enough, lad." He sat back in his swivel chair. He seemed to be at ease for the first time and smiled at Ollie. Then he wiped his eyeglasses.

"I went through Sandhurst, the English equivalent of West Point, you know. That's where I flunked flight training. When I graduated, the army did not need new infantry officers, so I got a job in the merchant marine. Then I signed on as a mercenary in North Africa. Dirty business, fighting Arabs in the desert. When war clouds started rising in 1937, I joined the army's special services outfit. And when war broke out they sent me to Oslo by fishing boat to make contacts, and several months later they parachuted me into Norway outside of Tromso where I froze my bloody balls off because spring came late that year. When I returned they put me in this job. That's it, son. Any more questions?"

"Yes, sir. When do I leave?"

"That depends on how your training goes. You'll just have to be patient. It will take us at least four months to train you so you'll be useful. And can survive," he added.

•••

"Can ya kill a mon?" Sergeant Angus McCloud demanded as he stared into the eyes of each of the six trainees standing at attention in front of him. "Can you kill? I hoop you won't have ta, but you better be tough. And ya better be able to kill." He glared at his recruits. "Are ya tough? Can you run five miles with a pack on your back? Can you climb a cliff or a tree?"

In turn each of the six stared back and answered the questions affirmatively. McCloud was only about five foot ten inches tall with strong tattooed arms and broad shoulders. A deep red scar ran down his face from below the left eye to the corner of his mouth. The scar gave him a cruel, angry look. "You will have to know how to live off the land. You will have to be able to win in hand-to-hand combat and you must be able to outsmart the enemy. And nivver forget that the fuckin' Germans are smart and ruthless. And I won't make you do anything I can't do, lads."

McCloud paused for what seemed to be a long time. "No one will know about your war for a long time. You will have to learn Norwegian and you will have to be alone for weeks on end. If any of you bastards want to quit," he growled, "better to get out now if you don't think you can do it. Just don't waste my time and quit in three months. If ya do that I'll maybe kill ya myself."

Ollie wondered what he had gotten into, but he was not about to let McCloud or his fellow trainees know that he had doubts, and that he was scared. He felt the sweat running down his armpits and his stomach was knotted. He had skied most of his life and was on the ski team at the University of Minnesota. He also had been on the freshman track team, so he thought he was in fairly good shape and he was going to show this damn sergeant how tough he was.

"Just to see how good shape you're in, lads, you are goin' ta run a mile now. Before we are done you'll run five miles with full packs on your bloody backs." McCloud warned the men again.

Next he made the trainees do forty pushups each. When they had stopped puffing air into their stinging lungs, McCloud made them stand at attention to hear him out.

"You all know about radios, but you'll become experts, and you'll learn codes, survival techniques, parachute jumping and handling explosives." Then looking at a blond man with a long nose and broad grin he said, "You, Carlson, come from Norway, so you skip the language classes, but instead you'll become a specialist in sinking small ships." Carlson grinned and McCloud shouted, "Take yer damn smile off," and the soldier looked at the ground, trying to hide the smile.

Two of the men were British, one was a Dane and one was from Canada. The Dane had been a schoolteacher and in England for a meeting when war began. He was a thin man with eyeglasses, and it soon became evident that he could not handle the physical pressure. McCloud sent him to Glasgow to a desk job.

Carlson, the Norwegian, seemed to have a perpetual smile. He had served in the Norwegian army, and come to Scotland with two cousins in a small sailboat when the Germans had invaded their country. Ollie found him friendly, but reserved. He told Ollie about his home in Alesund, where his father owned a small marina.

The two Brits had been raised in the slums of Southampton. They had joined the Navy together and had put in for transfer to special services because they wanted excitement. They both were lean and strong, and each wore a large black mustache. This almost caused a crisis when McCloud told them that they had to shave their whiskers, but he prevailed when he told them it was shave or be transferred to the infantry.

The sixth man was a jolly Canadian who at been a member of the Royal Canadian Mounties. At twenty-five, he was the oldest of the six recruits and his calm self-confidence proved to be catching. He and Ollie found they had much in common as two North Americans in a British operation.

True to his threat McCloud worked the men hard, increasing the distance they ran every day and adding packs after two months when their legs and backs had become tough. But he was not the only instructor. A small Japanese man taught Judo and he threw big Carlson to the ground with great ease as an example of how Judo could be used to defend oneself.

The third instructor was a gloomy Scotsman named Campbell, an expert in explosives. He also knew how to swim great distances in rubber wet suits. While the others studied language three hours a day, Campbell taught Carlson how to attach delayed action explosives to the hulls of boats.

Fortunately Ollie did not have to worry about swimming in freezing water, but he did learn how to blow up a bridge and warehouse. And he learned how to make a radio-controlled bomb explode.

As the weeks went by the five remaining trainees became a cohesive loyal company. When one of the Brits got into a scuffle in a pub because he tried to flirt with a young woman, her boyfriend got mad and the place erupted in a brawl. The trainees were outnumbered three to one. After thirty minutes however, when the police arrived, they had thoroughly beaten the locals. Using their Judo techniques they had disarmed two tipsy Scots who attacked with broken beer bottles.

McCloud was furious they had gotten into a fight and risked attracting attention. But then he told the men he was proud of them, although it took too long to win. And he was angry one of the Brits received a bloody nose in the brawl and Carlson hurt his hand when he missed with a punch and hit the wall instead. For his part, Ollie had knocked out one of the locals and bloodied the face of another, for which he received bruised knuckles.

"OK, lads," McCloud roared, no longer smiling. "Don't ivver do thot agin. We are not fightin' the local people. They are our friends, in case you bastards did not know it. We are fightin' the fuckin' Nazis. Just rememebr thot. Now ya'll run an extra mile to get the bad thoughts outta yer little heads. Do ya understand me? If any of you get into a fight with locals agin ya may find yerself in jail and I'll let ya rot in there."

After two months, a second group of trainees arrived and Ollie realized how much he had learned, how tough he had become, when he observed the newcomers.

During the third month the men were taken to mountainous country along the English border. There they were dropped off several miles apart. Each man carried a sleeping bag, ground cloth, food for two days, a compass and a hunting knife. That was all. They were to survive alone for four days and meet at a small lake twenty-seven miles away.

The instructors had taught them how to make a fire in the rain; how to minimize smoke; what berries could be eaten and which mushrooms were poisonous; how to make soup from plant leaves, roots, lichen, and wild animal bones; and finally how to trap a rabbit using a knife, twigs, string, and food.

Then came the big day, graduation. The men had looked forward to it for four tiring, often brutal months. Major Oglesby came to camp and gave each of them a certificate saying they had completed a special training program. Then he said, "Now you must return the letters for safe keeping. They will be sent to your homes after your mission is concluded. Until then, this program remains a secret. Talk about it even with friends and you endanger the lives of your comrades." He paused and looked at the five graduates and then concluded, "You each will be stationed in a small city on the western coast of Norway. Your only communication with the outside world will be by radio, but you will have to limit your transmissions so the Nazis can't find you. And you know each other and the new recruits, so you'll know who to trust, but trust no one else." With that the major took back the letters of commendation, and said, "Good luck and thank you." He got back in his jeep and was driven off. That was the last time Ollie saw him.

Ollie was brought back to reality when Erik pulled out a pipe, filled it carefully, cupped his hand against the wind and lit the tobacco. The smell of Erik's pipe tobacco was sweet, too sweet. Ollie felt his mouth watering with nausea. He wiped his forehead, which was beading with sweat.

"You look hungry, Olaf. Why don't you go below, warm up, and get something to eat," Erik said. "Gunnar has plenty of fish. You'll feel better with something in your stomach."

Ollie agreed, not for the chance of something to eat, but for the opportunity to warm up. His face and hands were numb and tingled when he reached the heat of the cabin. Sven, Ake, and the man Ollie had seen below deck before sat around the small table, drinking coffee and talking.

"Gunnar, get our new fisherman a bite to eat," Ake said, standing up and offering his chair to Ollie, who sat down.

"I don't need anything, really," Ollie said, rubbing his hands together.

"Eat while Sven and I check the net," Ake said.

The two men climbed the ladder as Gunnar went to the small stove and dished out fish stew, bread, cold ham, and cheese, which he gave to Ollie along with a cup of steaming black coffee.

"Really, I'm fine," Ollie said as Gunnar walked back to the galley and began rinsing tin bowls and cups in a bucket.

"Eat," Gunnar told him, swiping a gray rag inside a cup.

Ollie dipped his spoon into the bowl, pocked with rust spots. He lifted up a spoonful of stew, thick with chunks of fish, some pieces white, others brown. He felt the rush of saliva in his mouth again and his stomach tightening. He was hot and lightheaded. Dropping the spoon, he pushed himself from the table.

"You want seconds already?" Gunnar asked, turning as Ollie clambered up the ladder to the deck and the fresh, damp air that braced him momentarily.

He walked aft, where Ake and Sven were pulling a line through a winch, hauling in the net loaded with fish that they dumped into the storage hold. Ollie had never seen so many fish, flopping against each other like silver coins. The oily smell of the hold made his stomach even queasier. Suddenly he lunged for the port rail and threw up.

He stayed at the rail, embarrassed to move, to have Ake and Sven see him.

"We will make a fisherman of you yet, Olaf," Ollie heard Ake shout.

Sven walked over to Ollie. "Do not worry, we all did it once. You feel better?" he asked quietly, patting Ollie hard on the right shoulder before returning to help Ake.

"Much," Ollie mumbled, save for the taste in his mouth.

"You look like a new man," Erik said, clapping Ollie on the back.

Ollie wiped his mouth with his poncho sleeve. "I feel like one too," he said, holding tighter to the railing because his legs had gone rubbery. He definitely hadn't found his sea legs yet.

The two men watched the freighter as it sailed further away. With the net out of the water, the fishing boat began to increase its speed.

"We've picked a number of our Fishermen who are quick studies to train with you as radio operators," Erik began after awhile. "For a short time we could shuttle with some regularity from Bergen to the Shetland Islands, transporting messages about the Nazis and transporting our friends who were in danger. But the Germans are thick around here now and we need a faster and safer method of communication. A few months back one of our boats was sunk by the Nazi planes." Erik rubbed his forehead with his hands. "We lost a Fisherman."

"*Beklager*," Ollie said, offering his condolences. He remembered how Erik had earlier spoken of dying at sea in the frigid waters. A hell of a way to go.

Erik told him, "We have our hideout in back of a storage area above a restaurant owned by the father of one of our men, Thorvald. We call him Thor, after the Norse god of war. He's studying to be a lawyer. Late at night and in the morning we can work and not be concerned if we make noise because the Germans are usually not about. Thor's father gives us a signal when it's not safe. The Germans like the restaurant's food so at night they frequent the place. This is not an ideal arrangement but it's the best we have because we can see the harbor out of a small window and report on German shipments and other activity, as well as what they talk about when they drink too much at the restaurant."

Erik lit his pipe again. "We have two barns with supplies just outside of town where we can hide in an emergency and where we store some weapons. Usually two or three of us live above the restaurant, but sometimes we must be seen in Bergen to avoid suspicion. You will have to stay hidden because people will ask too many questions if a stranger is seen around for any length of time."

He became silent again and stared into the darkness. "I thought I saw a light starboard. Do you see anything?"

Ollie looked off to the right, aware that it was only a little after four in the afternoon but that night already had descended. He saw nothing, other than the rising black forms of waves cresting. "No lights," Ollie said.

"Maybe it was the moon breaking through the clouds for a moment," Erik said. "Or the Northern Lights. Or a ghost ship. They sink other ships and drown the sailors but no one knows exactly where the ships come from. Some believe that they're ships that were sunk in storms or in battle. Do you have ghost ships where you come from?"

"I've never heard of any ghost ships sailing around the lakes of Minnesota," Ollie said.

"Oh, Minnesota," Erik said. "There are a lot of Norwegian families there, I think," he told Ollie. "Do you have a Norwegian girl back home, Olaf?"

Ollie shook his head. "She wasn't Norwegian. She was fickle, though," he said, picturing Maryann with her flannel soft skin and gem green eyes. She had accepted the promise ring he gave her before he left for the University of Minnesota but mailed it back to him just two months later with a short note explaining how she wasn't ready for such a commitment. Maryann ended their relationship around the same time Ollie's grandmother received word about her sisters being taken to the Nazi camps. Up until that point Ollie had followed the belief that with work and effort, he could map the course of his life. But after Maryann left him, after he learned about his lost relatives, he discovered there wasn't just one, straight road to follow but many different and smaller paths that people were often forced to take. Ollie told Erik, "When we broke up, I quit school and joined the Canadians."

"So how did you get into a special operations services British unit?" Erik asked.

Ollie snorted. "Do you know the American slang, 'snafu?' It means 'situation normal all fucked up.' Some idiot in England got my records mixed up with a Canadian who was also named Olaf Larsen. And by the time anyone discovered the confusion I'd had two months of training and they decided to keep me."

As the boat plowed through the waves, Ollie told Erik a little about the training program that included classes in radio transmission, explosives, and a crash course in Norwegian. He was almost shouting to be heard over the increasing rain, the gusting wind and the smacking waves.

"You speak Norwegian well. For an American," Erik said with a grin.

Just then the boat slowed and changed course. "Evold knows more about the sea than any man I know, except maybe my father," Erik said as he motioned for Ollie to follow him. The two men walked back to the wheel-house, holding onto a thick rope strung from the stern to the ladder in order to make their way safely as the boat dove from one wave to the next.

"Blowing up more, Erik," Evold shouted. "I slowed again so the old girl doesn't take too much of a pounding. I think we should head in and get to the lee of the islands in case the storm gets much worse."

Erik nodded, then he and Evold looked at a map under glass near the wheel.

"We don't want to come too close to the islands up north, Olaf," Evold said, pointing to the chart. Ollie could see hundreds of small pinpoint dots in the blue water of the map. "There are too many islands and rocks. If we head northeast we should hit the mouth of the Hardangerefjord in about three hours. After that we can cruise behind the islands to protect ourselves from rough water all the way home."

"A good plan," Erik said. "And one that will keep Olaf from throwing up again."

"I don't think I have anything left to throw up," Ollie said.

"We'll fish again tomorrow until afternoon, then come in at dark," Erik said.

Ollie thought about another twenty-four hours in the smelly little boat that felt like it would either capsize or break apart at any second. Even though he had grown up in the land of a thousand lakes, Ollie had never taken to water, preferring solid and predictable ground beneath his feet. But in the military, he didn't have the luxury of choice. He did what he was told, like everyone else.

"Tomorrow we will catch many herring, you will see. We may be resistance fighters, but we are still fishermen," Evold said.

Erik went below deck to eat while Ollie stayed with Evold in the wheelhouse.

"Can you show me where we are?" Ollie shouted as he looked out at the rain and waves that hid any possible landmarks.

Evold traced a circle on the glass covering the map. "Somewhere here."

Ollie stared at the ferocious waves. Some of them he judged to be eight feet high, higher than anything he had seen in training. He wondered how Evold could steer and keep a course in such weather. "How well can you see?" he yelled.

"Hardly at all, but that's OK. I don't need to see. We are far from land still, yet too close for the big ships so it is a safe place to travel. I feel the boat. I judge the wind and waves. I listen in case I'm wrong and I watch my compass." Evold seemed relaxed and confident, his dark eyes staring alertly ahead despite the lack of visibility.

About an hour after Erik left the wheel, Sven came up with coffee to warm Ollie and Evold. The wheelhouse was crowded with the three of them inside so Ollie stood by the doorway. He took a gulp of the coffee and coughed before he had a chance to swallow. There was something more in the tin cup than just coffee.

"Spiked with aquavit," Evold said.

"Just a little," Sven told Ollie.

"Fights the cold," Evold added.

Just then the boat quivered as an unusually large wave broke over the rail, spilling a torrent of water across the boat and sweeping Ollie off his feet. He fell to the deck, the cup dropping from his hand, lost instantly in the rushing water. Ollie's fingers grasped for something, anything to hold onto. He felt himself slipping backwards along the deck, helplessly, until his arms snapped straight and he was pulled up onto his feet. In front of him stood Sven, behind him was the gunwale. Ollie coughed from the seawater that had filled his mouth and nose.

"We've all done this too," Sven said.

This time, with Sven still holding Ollie's wrists in a tight grip, Ollie understood that earlier in the day when they had shaken hands Sven wasn't trying to prove how tough he was. His small hands simply were tough, for which Ollie was particularly thankful just then.

"Take Olaf below, Sven," Evold yelled. "Before we lose him."

"How long could a man survive in that if he was washed overboard?" Ollie asked Sven as they leaned into the wind and walked toward the ladder.

"If he wasn't drowned first, maybe a man could survive for fifteen minutes," Sven said. "But he'd have to be strong and a good swimmer."

Ollie knew he was neither.

"Not even five minutes otherwise," Sven said. "Even in summer the water is cold in the North Sea."

Ollie realized how close he had come to being swept into the angry sea. It wasn't the way he wanted to die. Especially on the first day of his new assignment.

He knelt to climb down the ladder as Erik was climbing up. "It gets a little rough, eh?" Erik asked Ollie and Sven as he stepped onto the deck. "You will learn to love the sea," he told Ollie, slapping his back before Ollie went below.

Ake lay on one of the bunks, snoring. Gunnar sat at the table and smoked. Ollie and Sven hung up their rain gear on the pegs then sat with Gunnar as the boat began to toss even more wildly. "Cigarette?" Gunnar asked Ollie, who shook his head no. Smoking always made Ollie's throat sore. Sven lit a cigarette, the burning embers like an orange planet glowing in the dark universe.

Above them the wind shrieked like a nightmare ghost and the rigging knocked against the masts with thuds. Nearby the tin cups and plates rattled in the galley cupboard. Ollie was certain the boat would go over at any moment and if it did, he didn't want to be caught below. Another series of huge waves hit the boat, rolling it dangerously. Ollie grabbed onto the table. He felt himself panting. He couldn't let The Fishermen know that their operative from the British commando unit was scared shitless.

"On second thought," Ollie told Gunnar, "I'll take a smoke."

The three men smoked one, then two, then three cigarettes, the air turning gray like fog as the long winter night dragged on with no let up in the storm. Evold turned the boat south for an hour to reduce the roll. When the waves began to ease slightly, Erik changed course again and headed east. The storm continued, the boat rising high in the water only to crash down into troughs seconds later as if riding on the tracks of a giant roller coaster.

•••

Ollie woke with his head on his arms at the table and someone shaking his shoulder.

"*God morgen*," Erik said.

"*Ja*," Ollie said, sitting up and looking around. The berth was already empty of the others. He was stiff and sore and his throat hurt from smoking. His stomach was hollow. But he felt the boat sailing smoothly, as smoothly as a boat could on the open sea. The storm must have finally passed.

"We'll be in Bergen soon," Erik told him. "From now on, you must look and act like a fisherman." He fingered the sleeve of Ollie's blue sweater that the British had issued him. "Too new. Find a different sweater in the foot-locker," he said, pointing to a chest near the bunk where Ake had slept. "Then come above and swab the deck and wheelhouse. You'll need to keep to your business until we're sure the coast is clear and we can get you off the boat."

Ollie put on an old gray sweater and a black knitted cap, then found a mop and bucket and went above. Ake, Sven, and Gunnar were sitting in the stern and repairing the nets. Evold and Erik stood in the wheelhouse going over the charts.

The day was cold and drizzling but the waters were still compared to the night before. A light fog had settled over the coastline. As Erik steered the fishing boat, Ollie noticed seagulls flying a wide circle around the vessel, their screeching calls echoing in the low sky. A small white lighthouse nestled in an outcropping of rocks shone its yellow rotating beam through the mist. Soon Ollie saw what he gathered was Bergen, a village of tile-roofed houses painted bright red, yellow, and white that stair-stepped up the slopes of the surrounding hills that were veiled with low clouds.

While the fish-laden boat slowed to pull into Vaagen, the harbor, Ollie began scrubbing the deck. Erik steered the boat close to the dock and Gunnar jumped down to the landing. Ake tossed him the bowline that Gunnar wrapped around a thick wood post, mooring the boat.

There were a few other fishing boats tied up at Bryggen, the quay, and several fishermen were on the decks unloading barrels of fish, checking sails, and oiling winches. The nearby street was mostly empty except for a few people traveling on bikes and others walking with cloth sacks of food or brown paper-wrapped packages. The scene looked like a primitive painting of a small town, peaceful and innocent, Ollie thought, save for the small group of German soldiers that he could see walking a few blocks away.

As Ollie continued pushing the mop back and forth, back and forth, the gray mop strings extending across the weathered wood deck like octopus tentacles, he heard a man call Gunnar's name. He glanced over and saw two more tall men, one with round wire-rimmed glasses, the other red-haired and wearing a heavy green jacket buttoned to the neck. The men stopped to talk with Gunnar, who handed them cigarettes. The three leaned their heads together, the pair lighting their cigarettes off the end of Gunnar's. Then Gunnar shook hands with the men before the two left, walking in the direction of the German soldiers down the quay. Gunnar turned and flicked his cigarette into the water.

Erik walked quickly to Ollie. "We go now, Olaf," he said, motioning with his index finger to Sven and Ake to join them. "You take over where Olaf left off," he told Sven, who took the mop from Ollie. "Ake come with me."

The three men jumped to the dock. When Ollie landed he felt dizzy, the ground seeming to roll beneath his feet like the boat. He spread his legs apart and held his arms slightly out to his sides, ready to break his fall if he tipped over.

"Thor and Karl said that a German patrol passed a few minutes earlier and would not be back for at least fifteen minutes," Gunnar told them.

"You stay with the cargo, Gunnar," Erik said. "Ake and I will take Olaf to the hideout."

"If anyone asks, Olaf, we are just three fishermen on our way to breakfast," Ake said as he, Erik, and Ollie began walking along the cobblestones toward a row of old wooden buildings. Ollie found it hard to keep up with the others, forcing himself to move faster, his legs feeling thick and uncooperative, and his footing even more unsure on the rough stones. If the Germans returned sooner than expected, he didn't want to call attention to himself by lagging behind, to appear any different from Erik and Ake. So he pressed on with the two men to a narrow alley between the buildings.

A stooped older man with a hand-hewn cane emerged from a doorway.

"All clear in back, but there's two of them downstairs in the restaurant," he whispered in passing.

"Hurry," Erik said as they hustled through the alley to the back of one of the buildings. "Be quiet now," he told them before they started climbing an old wooden exterior staircase, dry-rotted in spots, which rattled and moaned beneath their footsteps up to the third floor.

Ake opened the door and they entered what seemed to be an unused apartment that also served as a storage room. The room was lit by a dim bulb and contained a refrigerator with a rusting door, five wooden chairs with broken caning stacked on top of one another, a tall chest of drawers, a metal bed frame, and cases of canned food, everything covered with a gray film of dust. Ollie could smell grease and cooked cabbage seeping up from the restaurant below and realized he would be living with the stench for months to come.

Erik walked to the dresser. He knocked softly against the wall behind the dresser three times, then he knocked again once. "The door is booby trapped against a surprise raid," he told Ollie before knocking one more time again. "We'll teach you the disarm code so you don't blow up yourself and everything else on the block," he said as the dresser rolled out from the wall, revealing a hidden doorway.

A tall handsome man with blond curly hair, deep blue eyes and a broad smile stood on the other side of the wall. Erik ducked and stepped through the passageway. Ake and Ollie followed him into the small hideout that had a high ceiling, a small dormer window covered with a muslin curtain, two narrow beds folded up against a wall, a table, and two upholstered chairs.

The tall man gently pulled the dresser shut behind them.

"This is Valdy, the Norwegian cross country ski champion. If there had been a 1940 Olympics, he would have won," Erik said softly to Ollie.

Valdy chuckled. "Nei, there would have been other good skiers, but maybe," he said.

"I'm Olaf," Ollie said, shaking Valdy's hand.

"We are glad you are safe," he said. " We were worried. We heard about the storm. All the fishermen are saying it was the worst so far this year."

"Olaf was not scared," Ake said, snickering.

Ollie shook his head while Erik added, "He's a good man, for a landlubber."

"You are named after one of Norway's great heroes, King Olav, Olaf Tryggvason. History tells us that he once climbed an 800-foot cliff near Maloy. And they did not have rock climbing equipment in those ancient days. He also was famous because he was the Viking chief who led the invasion of England around the year 1000. But most importantly," Valdy laughed, "he was the man who founded Bergen. So you have a perfect name for our city." He patted Ollie's back and added, "I like your face, Olaf."

"Thank you, Valdy. I appreciate the history lesson," Ollie said.

Later, after Erik and Ake pulled the beds down from the wall to rest and Valdy left to bring back food for the men, Ollie stood at the small window, peering out the glass from behind the curtain. He could see the quay and Erik's fishing boat. He watched as an older model truck drove up to the dock and parked beside the boat. Two young men stepped out and one of them put his fingers to his mouth and looked as though he was whistling. Soon Sven and Gunnar appeared on deck. They handed off the barrels of fish and Ollie's hidden radio equipment and munitions to the two men, who loaded the cargo onto the truck's bed. Ollie knew from Erik that the barrels would be driven to Eduard's warehouse a few blocks west along the harbor, where the barrels would be unloaded by other members of the underground. From there the equipment and munitions would be repackaged into canned food boxes that would be delivered to the restaurant and smuggled up to Ollie in the hideout, one box at a time, over a four-day and night period. Then Ollie could begin his real work.

chapter two

OLLIE LARSEN, ESQ., sat in his comfortable upholstered desk chair, looking out his 25th floor window at the Golden Gate Bridge. It was a scene he loved, and whenever he was trying to determine his options in a difficult case he told his secretary, Laura, to hold calls while he sat and looked at the bay.

After almost an hour of calm thinking he buzzed her to come in. "Laura, ask Cindy and Rob to bring me their files on the utility case. I can't stall any longer if we're going to get our briefs ready for the Supreme Court dead-line." He still had mixed feelings about being involved in the case, but the utilities had been clients of theirs for more than twelve years so he figured he owed them the firm's best shot.

The case involved California ratepayers suing the utilities for millions of dollars, claiming they had been over-charged. Ollie's senior partners had been divided after losing in the lower courts. Two felt it was their duty to represent their client right or wrong. The other two said that the power companies were dishonest and it would be morally wrong to take the case. Reluctantly, Ollie decided that the firm had to handle the appeal. It would bring in a huge fee and win much good publicity in the profession. In addition, it would be a great challenge arguing before the Supreme Court if the justices accepted the case on their calendar.

That had been his reasoning. He still was not happy or comfortable with the case, but the idea of going before the Supreme Court again was too enticing to resist. When the two junior partners, Cindy and Rob, came into his office, Ollie listened to their reports with his eyes closed. Then he asked questions about how the rates had been set, what additional income would be derived, and how many depositions might be needed.

"What do you know about the new lawyers added to the legal team representing the ratepayers?" Ollie asked. "I hear they're young."

Cindy and Rob looked at each other, as if the other had been responsible for gathering the information.

"Not a lot," Cindy told him, tapping her pen on the arm of the chair.

"But we'll find out," Rob said, making a note on his legal pad.

They were young, too, but driven. It had been a year or so since Ollie had stumped one of them with a question, but he still liked to try.

They continued discussing details about the case until Laura, a plump middle-aged woman with dyed blond hair, interrupted the three. "Mr. Larsen," she began tentatively, "I know you don't want to be disturbed but this cable just arrived from Norway. I thought it might be important." She handed Ollie the cable and stood waiting for instructions. Ollie felt the two young lawyers watching him as he opened the yellow envelope. He silently read the telegram: "Biggest fish in Bergen. Need you to land him. Remember oath. Everything ready. Come soon. — Erik" Ollie's face flushed as he folded the cable and, with trembling hands, shoved it inside the envelope.

"Are you all right?" Cindy asked.

"Yes," Ollie replied softly. "It's just a message from an old friend, from the military."

He put the envelope in his desk drawer to read again when he was alone, without his two young assistants and Laura, who had worked with him for almost twenty years, present. His staff knew that Ollie had been in a special military operation in Norway during World War II and had been captured by the Germans, but that was all he had ever said about it except to his most senior partner, Walter, who had served in the Pacific theater.

With Erik Nestvold's message in his desk, Ollie found it hard to concentrate on the case. He looked out the window and as he did so he could picture the harbor in Bergen, or at least the part he had seen. Except for a few fishing boats and some German naval patrol gunboats, the Bergen harbor had been relatively quiet when he had been there. Certainly it did not look like busy San Francisco Bay with its beautiful bridge, large freighters, and spotless cruise ships. Ollie kept thinking about Bergen and Erik and he could not clear his mind.

Even if Erik was correct, could Ollie really take time off with a major case coming up? And how could he be certain that Erik was right? After all, the man was a hot head and a storyteller. How could Ollie check the veracity of the message? He had kept in touch a bit with Thorvald. Maybe he should telephone Thor and ask what he thought. After all, he was reliable and loyal, he was intelligent and trustworthy. Thor and Erik were Ollie's closest surviving friends, men he had stayed in touch with periodically over the years through the occasional letter or Christmas card.

Except, did he really want to have a reunion in Norway? Could he go back to a place where he had experienced so much pain? He had tried to put the war far in his past. Now the past might be resurrected in the present more than fifty years later. He had been only twenty-one years old when he had landed in Norway, and now he was in his mid-seventies, a successful California corporate lawyer with three children and five grandchildren. He had a condo in Vail where he, his wife Polly, and the rest of the family went skiing every winter. Even though he could well afford to, he'd never returned to Europe, not even to receive medals from the Norwegian government for meritorious service. He'd asked that the medals be sent through the mail. So much had happened in Norway that he didn't want to relive and remember. Although he'd hardly been able to forget. Especially on cold, damp days when his hands ached from the torture and he thought of Kraus. The squinting eyes. The tight mouth. The ratchet laugh. The old hatred still boiled up easily, even after all the years. Yet he could not go back to Norway, especially if it meant jeopardizing everything he'd achieved for a crazy mission of revenge.

But Ollie had taken the oath. Erik, Thorvald, Valdy, and Sven had come to see him on Ollie's last night in Bergen. The five men each had cut a finger and put their blood on a Bible. Then they had sworn to take revenge on Kraus if it was the last thing they did. Now Valdy and Sven were dead, but what of Kraus? Was he still alive? And was Ollie still morally bound to that old oath, or had time and circumstances freed him?

Perhaps returning to Bergen only to try to dissuade Erik and the others from doing anything rash could fulfill his obligation. And because he'd always followed Polonius' advice in *Hamlet*, to be true to himself even when some persistent part of him fought for escape from reality, the truth was that he admitted the possibility of seeing Kirsten again. Not out loud. Certainly not to Polly. He'd talked little about his wartime experiences in Norway with his wife. He'd never told her about Kirsten. But he'd long wondered what had happened to her, and if she was even still alive.

For four days the letter remained untouched in Ollie's desk. But every so often it seemed he could feel the message from the tissue-thin paper pressing on his fingertips. After all, these were men who had risked their lives for him; others who had died because of him. He realized he needed to go.

"Last I heard only eleven of the original twenty-five Fishermen are still alive and healthy," he told Polly on the fourth night. "God, they're old men."

Polly walked over to where Ollie stood looking out his picture window at the water in the Bay. She patted his soft stomach and kissed his temple before handing him his martini. They were relaxing, listening to the CDs she put on as she did most every evening.

Ollie stiffened as he heard the great chords introducing Beethoven's *Fifth Symphony*. He had never realized how much they sounded like the letters "s" and "t" from the Morse code—dot dot dot dash—the method of communication that he and the other underground groups had used to send messages to the British about the Germans. He had sat for hours in a wooden, straight-back chair during 1941 and 1942, listening intently through headphones as he sent and received the staccato choruses of letters and numbers that formed the relayed information.

As Ollie watched the sun settle into the horizon, seeming to set the ocean on fire, he was stirred by the Beethoven piece. He could feel again those moments on a hill behind Bergen after he and several other Fishermen had repaired a hidden transmitter and started back down. They had to dodge from tree to tree and rock to rock to escape detection. At one point Ollie had looked out over Bergen's harbor at the magnificence of a similarly fiery sunset and felt at peace for a brief second, the war forgotten, and the approaching German patrol unseen.

Now all these years later, he felt a moment of panic. He took a long swallow of his cocktail, letting the alcohol burn his throat.

"Welcome back," Polly said softly, putting her arms around him. "Where have you been?"

He shook his head to clear it and gave her a half-smile.

"Exactly what did Erik say?" she asked.

Ollie had read the letter just once, but he remembered it word for word and recited it to her.

"The big fish," Polly said, sighing. "The one that got away." Ollie had told her just enough about what had happened to him so that she knew about Kraus.

She rested her head on his shoulder and they watched the Bay in silence. Finally she said, "Don't go, Ollie. They can do whatever they want without you. You were almost killed helping them, wasn't that enough?"

When he didn't answer she walked away. Slowly the sun sank into the ocean. It was the beauty of this that made his eyes sting and water. Polly brought him another martini and sat down on the couch, sipping her own. The evening grew dark and distant lights created a silhouette of the hilly city.

He turned to her. "Come with me," he said.

She shook her head. "This isn't a vacation that you're going on," she said, never taking her eyes off the exquisite panorama in front of them. "It's better if I stay at home."

Ollie let his breath out slowly, hoping she wouldn't sense his relief. He didn't want her mixed up in whatever it was the lunatic Fishermen were concocting. If he couldn't contain them, the whole thing could blow up into something dangerous, something a lawyer of his standing should avoid at all costs, should stay six thousand miles away from at his comfortable home, in his comfortable life, with a wife he'd adored for fifty-two years, whose husband all of a sudden felt a confusion so deep he wondered if air would ever find its way back into his lungs again.

...

As the plane broke through the last layer of clouds, Ollie could see Vaagen, the Bergen harbor, where two modern ocean liners were tied up and a tanker was taking on North Sea oil. They were surrounded by dozens of fishing, sail and powerboats—looking so tiny and toy-like next to the large ocean-going vessels. Every so often, a ray of sun split the gray sky and sparkled on the water. The city nestled under low mountains covered with green pine. He saw the old wooden buildings that flanked one side of the harbor. He remembered they dated back to the days of the fourteenth century Hanseatic League, when the free towns of Norway and northern Germany formed an association for trade and protection. Now the buildings looked even older when compared with nearby post-war concrete and steel office buildings.

It was a peaceful, idyllic scene from the air, not like that cold bleak day of late November 1941 when he had sailed through the outer islands, past the rock jetty entrance and into the harbor with Erik and his small crew. Mysteriously, the smell of the fishing boat—dirty and crammed with its catch of halibut and herring—seemed to fill the plane's cabin. The memory of the odor was so real that Ollie had to shake his head and look around the cabin to remind himself he was flying first class on a clean SAS DC-9. He inhaled deeply and for once was glad for the slightly musty smell of recycled airplane air. There were only a few things that would ever have brought him back to Bergen, to the memories that made the odor of a fishing boat so long ago send his heart racing now.

The plane circled over the tall forest-covered hills as it made its final approach. He tightened his seat belt. He had cabled Erik with information about his arrival time. Erik had cabled back that he would make all the necessary arrangements, including meeting him at the airport. In a few minutes he would be welcomed by Erik the giant. During his stay he no doubt would see some of the other Fishermen, too. And he allowed himself the possibility of looking up Kirsten.

The plane touched down so softly that Ollie hardly realized they were on the ground. Off to the side of the airfield he could see the towering Norway spruce that had been used in early times to build the great Viking ships. The airliner taxied down the runway toward a modern terminal. Change number one, Ollie thought, as he peered out the window at the light green glass facade.

Ollie stayed seated as the others around him stood quickly to retrieve their bags and other belongings. The passengers soon crowded into the aisle, pressing against one another, impatient for the door to open. Ollie waited. Even though his journey had been long—eighteen hours and three different planes—he felt as though the plane had arrived too quickly, before he was ready. He saw a flight attendant open the door and watched his fellow travelers begin to move forward to vacations or business or home. His mission was of a different sort, one he was still unsure of. He wasn't even sure how long it would last. Erik had told him to make his return ticket open-ended.

As the disembarking passengers dwindled, a young flight attendant with white-blonde hair and high cheekbones saw Ollie in his seat. "Do you need assistance, sir?" she asked him in English with a rolling cadence. "I can call for a wheelchair."

Ollie shook his head and said, "No, no, I'm fine. " He laughed. "Jet lag," he claimed as he stood and opened and closed his stiff hands before reaching for his briefcase and overnight bag in the overhead compartment.

He walked down the jetway and through the gate and stood in line at customs. Beyond the customs agents' booths was a wall with Plexiglass windows that cordoned off arriving passengers from the main terminal. People waited on the other side and every now and then Ollie heard some-one yelling greetings to a person who had just passed through customs. Ollie tried to look for Erik but the overhead lights glared off the Plexiglass and he could make out only silhouettes.

When it was his turn, Ollie handed his passport to the customs agent who stamped a page. Then he was on his way through a turnstile to the concourse.

Ollie saw the giant immediately. There could be no mistake. Despite deep lines in his leathery face and red hair that had grown silver, Erik was unmis-takable, towering over everyone else, although now he was slightly stooped. He was dressed in a wrinkled gray suit that was tight around his ample middle and on his head was an old black fishing cap. Under his suit coat he wore a turtle neck sweater even though it was a summer day. A big smile spread across Erik's huge face as Ollie walked toward him.

"*Velkommen, velkommen,* I am Erik the Red. I hope you like fishing in Norway," Erik said in Norwegian.

Ollie laughed. "I am Olaf the Viking. I come to bring fish to market," Ollie replied, giving the old code words, only in English this time. They grabbed each other in a bear hug.

"Ollie, my old friend," Erik roared, also in English.

"Erik, you big crazy Viking."

They kissed each other's cheeks and hugged again. Then Ollie heard a high-pitched voice calling, *"Velkommen, velkommen,"* from behind Erik.

Ollie stepped back and saw a short old man in a bright gold jacket and light blue pants, wearing brown-tinted glasses, his thinning hair combed from back to front over a bald spot. "You have finally returned, Olaf," the man said in halting English, smiling all the while. He had a gold tooth.

"Ake," Ollie shouted as he wrapped the little man in a big hug. Ake's once powerful shoulders were sloped, his back bony, and his muscles soft and small.

"Oh, Olaf, it is good to see you back here again," Ake said.

"My turn," Ollie heard someone with a deep voice say. He looked up and saw Thor, wearing round wire-rimmed glasses, his hair a silver gray but still as thick as it was years before. He held out his hands to Ollie, the knuckles knobbed with arthritis like barnacles on a ship. "My friend," he said, holding Ollie tight.

Ollie patted Thor's back, still strong and broad. He hadn't known how much he missed these men all this time.

A tall thin man with thick glasses and a bald head stepped up beside Thor and held out his hand shyly. Ollie tried to remember who he was.

"Velkommen, old friend. Have you forgotten me? I am Evold," the man told him, also in English.

In the older man, Ollie gradually recognized the features of the strong, quiet, ruddy boat captain of half a century earlier. Back then Evold's hair had been a wild black shrub and his shoulders were so wide that, if he was not careful, he sometimes bumped the doorframe when walking into the hide-out. Now he wore thick eyeglasses that he hadn't needed when he stood in the small wheelhouse of the fishing boat, peering out at the mysterious ship in the fog. And he was thin, with a familiar yellow cast to his skin, just like a friend back home who had cancer.

"Evold, of course I remember you. How could I ever forget you? You helped me escape." Ollie hugged him, too.

When Evold released him, Ollie squeezed Evold's hand, as if he could pass along some of his own strength to buoy Evold through the challenges ahead.

And then Ollie was surrounded and hugged by more men from the old days, as well as their wives, children, and grandchildren. It seemed that the airport was full of Norwegians who were there for the specific purpose of welcoming Ollie back to their country.

Suddenly Erik raised his hands and the whole crowd stood at attention and began singing a spirited version of the Norwegian national anthem. They followed with a thoroughly off-key, but lusty rendition of the Star Spangled Banner, much to the amusement of the few other people still in the concourse. When the singing and cheering concluded, Erik climbed on a chair, raising him even higher above the crowd.

"My friends," he roared in the deep voice Ollie remembered so well, "our old friend, Olaf, the American Viking, has returned to Bergen. We have not forgotten how he risked his life for our beloved Norway in her darkest hours of need. Olaf, we look forward to showing you our beautiful city, which you helped to save, and having many big parties with drink and food to honor you. And we will also take you fishing again, which we remember you enjoyed so well."

He paused and everyone laughed as Ollie shook his head. "Thank you for coming back, dear friend," Erik said. "*Velkommen*, again, to Bergen."

As the crowd clapped, Ollie climbed on a nearby chair. "My old fishing friends and your families, thank you, *takk*. I never expected such a *velkommen*," he said, trying to use as many Norwegian words as he could remember. "It is so good to be back with my old comrades, my brothers who fought so bravely and so alone, and who helped to save the world from Nazi tyranny. We have much to catch up on and stories to tell in the next few days, so for now all I can say is thank you so much. *Takk so mikka*."

While they waited for luggage to arrive on the carousel, Ollie looked around at members of the group with mixed emotions. His brave war time comrades had grown old, older than he expected. Some of them obviously were not well. He was especially saddened looking at little Ake and the once handsome Evold. Others, however, still appeared vigorous, especially Thorvald, with whom he had shared a passion for talking about philosophies, economics and political theories.

Erik stood beside him and asked, "What color is your suitcase?" as the bags began tumbling down the carousel.

"Black," Ollie replied.

"Good one," Erik said, laughing.

Ollie looked at the luggage rotating in front of them. All but one were black. "With wheels," Ollie said. "I'll know it when I see it."

"We have made you a reservation at the new SAS Hotel by the harbor for a night," Erik told him. "From there you will have a fine view which you did not have in the old days." He laughed again. "Then my older daughter and her family go back to Oslo and you move into my guest room so we can visit. It is much different from the old guest room you lived in the last time you were in Bergen."

The two men snorted, sharing the memory of the small secret room in which the underground radio had been located. Four Norwegians took turns staying in the hideout above the restaurant with Ollie. He taught them how to set up the equipment, send and receive messages, and how to repair the radio — especially how to repair the radio, which always seemed to be breaking down.

"I couldn't impose on your wife, Erik," Ollie answered. "I'll stay at the hotel."

"No, no, my friend, you stay with me for two reasons. Olga would have her feelings hurt if you stayed at the hotel. Also, the hotel is booked beginning tomorrow with many people in town for a big cable TV station dedication that we will be attending. No rooms are available." Erik grinned. "So you have to be our guest."

Ollie smiled and agreed. Then he saw his bag. As he started to reach for the handle, Erik's hand swooped down like a seagull and lifted the suitcase before Ollie had a chance.

"Listen, Erik," Ollie said quietly, resting his hand on Erik's forearm. "What about landing the big fish?"

Erik shook his head. "No, no, we don't speak of that today. Fishing is later. First I'll take you to your hotel so you can rest. Then I have planned a big party so you can catch up with the rest of The Fishermen."

Ollie understood right then that Erik had scheduled practically each minute of his visit and that he would do best to follow the giant's orders, just as he had more than fifty years before.

chapter three

OLLIE WAS ALONE in his clean and simple hotel room. At last. The pleasure of seeing his friends had, for a while, delayed the rush of exhaustion that hit him now. He stood at the window looking out at the busy harbor with its small boats, mammoth ocean-going freighters, and sleek tourist liners that took foreigners to see the beautiful northern fjords, before he closed the drapes to shut out the daylight. Then he sat on the bed and dialed Polly long distance, as he promised her he'd do each day.

It was after midnight in San Francisco, but she picked up after the first ring as if she had been waiting beside the phone. "Ollie?" she asked, her voice hoarse from sleep. He imagined what she looked like in their bed, her hair thick and loose, her arms bare, her skin smelling sweet and flowery with night cream.

"I've made it," he said, then gave her the hotel's phone number and his room number. "I won't keep you," he told her.

"No, no, I'm glad you called," she said. He thought he could hear her yawning.

"Sweet dreams," he said.

"Be careful," she told him.

After he hung up the phone Ollie lay down on top of the spread, with his right arm resting over his eyes, to nap for fifteen minutes. Just enough to combat the jet lag, but not long enough to keep him on San Francisco time. The room's drapes eliminated the light but not the sounds around him. He heard car engines, a jackhammer at work, voices in the hotel hallway.

And then the phone.

Ollie rolled over and looked at the clock. He had been asleep for more than two hours. He picked up the receiver.

"Hello, Olaf. We are here," Erik's voice boomed over the line.

"I'll be down in fifteen minutes," Ollie answered.

After a quick shower Ollie dressed and shaved hurriedly and took the elevator to the brightly lit lobby. There he found Erik, Ake, Thor, and a short, squat woman with her blonde hair twisted into a thick bun.

"My wife, Signe," Thor said.

"Pleasure," Ollie told her as Signe stood on tiptoes to kiss him on both cheeks.

"An honor," she said.

The group crowded into Erik's small and shiny Saab. Signe sat in the front passenger seat while Ollie and Thor sat in back with Ake on Thor's lap. Erik and Signe competed as tour guides, describing everything they passed, while Erik drove slowly along the quay.

Suddenly Erik slammed on the brakes, nearly getting the Saab rear-ended by a driver who sounded his horn. Erik rolled down his window and motioned for the other car to pass, which it did, horn continuing to blare. Ake giggled.

"Do you know what that is, Olaf?" Erik asked, pointing to a red-painted wooden building.

Ollie looked at the structure. On the ground floor was a restaurant with an outdoor patio filled with tables, bright blue striped umbrellas, and chairs. Ollie turned around and looked at the harbor, at the view he had so often seen those many years before. "That was our hideout, wasn't it?" he said.

"Now the room is a museum honoring the underground resistance. We are very proud of it," Signe told him.

"I will take you there tomorrow, Olaf," Thor said, "if I can steal you away from Erik."

"Ja, I suppose. I have nothing planned for Olaf until late afternoon. You can help him check out of the hotel, then do as you wish," Erik said, starting to drive the car again along the quay, past the busy fish market where Ollie could see dozens of people buying everything from salmon to eels, and where tourists purchased troll figurines along with the usual trinkets, T-shirts and caps. Erik turned on a side street, taking them past a beautiful old church with a high spire that towered over the harbor and nearby buildings.

"What's that called?" Ollie asked.

"Nykirken," Thor said. "It was damaged during the war but completely restored afterwards."

From there Erik drove Ollie by Den National Scene, the theater located in an art nouveau building, and Hoyskolen i Bergen, the university. The whole time, Erik and Signe gestured right then left, pointing out other landmarks to Ollie as they snaked their way up a small mountain, high above the town.

Erik pulled in the driveway of a two-story pink house.

"Welcome to the Nestvold estate," Erik said, laughing, as the group opened the Saab's doors and everyone stepped out of the car.

Ollie stood for a moment, taking in the view of the harbor that was clear and spectacular. He could see for miles out to sea, including several green islands on the horizon. From the hideout in the old days, his view was confined to just the inner harbor and the breakwater.

"We think we have the most beautiful city in the world," Signe said, patting her hair and straightening her skirt.

"I can't argue," Ollie told her.

"This way," Erik said, taking Ollie by the arm. They walked toward the outside stairs of the house with Ake, Thor, and Signe following them. Over the front door Ollie saw a large sign that read, "Oensk Olaf Velkommen, Viking," flanked by Norwegian and American flags.

Erik whistled, and a crowd of people poured out the door and onto the steps, shouting, "*Velkommen, velkommen.*"

Ollie felt his face redden, unexpectedly. He hadn't blushed since he was a young man. But there in front of all these people shaking his hands and hugging him as he walked by, he was overwhelmed. He recognized a few guests—Eduard, who still owned the fish warehouse; Rolf, who had been a piano student during the occupation and afterwards became a music professor; and Lars, who still ran, mostly marathons and was ranked fifth in his age group in the whole of Norway—but most he didn't know, especially the younger ones. Children and grandchildren of the men he served with, no doubt. He was ushered into Erik's house, as if on a wave.

The living room was spacious, with white walls covered by several dozen photographs of Erik's family, fishing boats and the Norwegian fjords. In the center of the room was a huge table laden with varieties of herring, smoked salmon, cheese, pickles, hams, jams, cakes, breads, and salads. At one end were dozens of bottles of aquavit and beer.

The table was presided over by a tall, tanned woman with aquamarine eyes. "At last I meet my husband's dear American friend," she said, giving Ollie a long hug and kissing his cheeks.

"Olaf, my wife Olga loves you, so I am jealous," Erik shouted, grabbing Ollie's arm. "Meet the rest of my family before Olga runs away with you."

Erik led Ollie to a beautiful, auburn-haired young woman who gave Ollie a warm smile. "My younger daughter, Orla," Erik said.

Ollie felt his breath catch. For a moment he thought she was Kirsten. Stupid, he thought, shaking his head ever so slightly. Kirsten would be well into her seventies by now and the woman in front of him was in her thirties. He took a deep breath and held out his hand to her. "Good to meet you," he said as she gently shook his hand.

"And here is my older daughter, Clara, and my youngest grandchildren, Annie and Arne," Erik said. The children smiled shyly and made formal bows to Ollie, who shook their hands too.

Two tall young men, almost as large as their father, were next introduced. "Jens Christian. He is named after the national commander of the Milorg resistance forces during the war, Jens Christian Hauge," Erik said. "And this one is Erik Olaf." Erik and his son both smiled at Ollie.

It took only a second for Ollie to realize the young man had been named after him. "I'm speechless and honored," he said as the two sons pumped his hand vigorously. He thought of his own children, named after beloved relatives. And now his name was a part of Erik's lineage. "You never told me," he said to Erik.

"Family secret," Erik said.

"You have a handsome brood. Lucky they don't look like you," Ollie teased.

At that moment, a stocky, red-haired man wearing a dark business suit with a bright red necktie burst through the door. "*Trist! Jeg er sen*," he shouted, waving at Ollie. "*Olaf, hus meg?*"

"Olaf's Norwegian is a little rusty," Erik told the man.

"Remember me, Olaf?" the man asked in English.

Ollie stared at the newcomer, trying to make the connection but without success.

"I'm Kris," the man said with a smile that displayed a perfect set of white teeth.

"Kristian, my star pupil," Ollie said, finally recognizing the youngest of The Fishermen, who had been only sixteen when he joined the group as a courier. He dressed all in black and carried messages to the hideout, sneaking through back alleys at night, avoiding the Germans with amazing ingenuity while taking daring risks. After delivering messages, Kris would watch Ollie work for hours. He learned Morse code by himself, through observing Ollie. Ollie had quickly realized that the boy possessed an inquisitive mind that could be easily trained. He taught him to put together radios and send messages. And here he was all these years later.

"I'll never forget the first time you saw me," Kris said. "You thought I was too young to help The Fishermen."

"You were!" Ollie said.

"You were only five or six years older!" Kris said.

"Seemed like more at the time," Ollie told him.

"Thanks to your training I was able to open a small radio store after the war," Kris said. "I went to business school, too. Then I opened another store. Now I have eight stores in cities from Bergen all the way to Kirkenes at the northern tip of Norway. We sell radios, televisions, stereos, cell phones and appliances," he said. "And next year we will start selling computers."

"I'm happy for you Kris," Ollie replied, giving his former protege a bear hug and a slap on the back. "I have a friend who I think still lives in Kirkenes that I was thinking of looking up while I was here."

"It's far north," Kris said. "But I could take you there in my plane."

"Oh, it's probably too much trouble," Ollie said. "I think Erik has my days scheduled full anyway."

"Nonsense," Kris told him. "If you want to visit a friend while you're here, you should visit a friend while you're here."

Ollie looked up at the ceiling, thinking. He'd only halfheartedly mentioned going to Kirkenes to see Kirsten, and here was Kris offering Ollie the use of his plane to actually make the trip. Could he really go there? "Let's see then," Ollie said.

By the end of their conversation the room was crowded and noisy. Ollie circulated among the group, talking with everyone, drinking beer and nibbling on food with his comrades as they tried to catch up on one another's lives. He learned from Thor that, after serving for a number of years as a prosecutor, he was nearly retired from the small law firm he had set up with his brother nearly thirty years before, spending most of his time teaching a class at the university and writing poetry. Ollie saw big Nils, who had gone completely bald, his head shiny and smooth. He was still a fisherman. And Gunnar, whose shoulders were just as wide and strong, and whose hobby was woodworking. Chairs were his specialty.

After several hours Erik climbed partway up the staircase to the second floor. "My dear friends," he roared, his face even redder from the drinks he'd consumed. "We must drink a toast," he said, as the room quieted. Someone handed Ollie a glass of aquavit. "Let us drink to America and Britain for helping us win the war, and let us drink to our very special old friend, Olaf the Viking."

Everyone cheered, and Ollie felt the powerful liquor burn his throat as he drained the glass in one big gulp. Someone refilled his glass, and he climbed up next to Erik.

"My friends, my dear, dear friends, this is one of the happiest moments of my life. I would like to drink to my adopted country, Norway," he said.

The guests cheered loudly.

"And I wish to toast all of you, and the memory of our brave comrades who are no longer with us," Ollie told them, raising his glass as the others clinked theirs together.

"And to justice for that bastard Kraus," Erik said, flinging his glass to the stairs where it broke into sequin-sized shards. "May he get what he deserves."

"Erik Nestvold," Olga murmured.

"Hush now," Thor warned Erik as he strode toward him, taking Erik by the arm and leading him down the steps. Ollie followed as Olga hurried to the staircase with napkins in her hands to sweep up the pieces of glass.

"Drink. Eat," she told the guests, who had quieted. Ollie felt the group staring as he and Thor escorted Erik from the living room.

"Not here," Thor said softly, looking hard at Erik. "Don't mention his name again."

"I'm sorry," Erik whispered while they walked to a back hallway.

"It's all right," Ollie said. "I feel the same way."

"I'm sorry," Erik said again before what seemed like a great laugh burst from his mouth, only just at the end the sound turned heavy and choked. He leaned over, his hands covering his face, his shoulders beginning to heave up and down with sobs.

"I'm sorry too," Ollie said, kneeling beside him.

"We all are," Thor said, placing his hand on Erik's back.

They helped Erik to the bathroom where he splashed his face with cold water, and soon the men rejoined the party. By the end of the evening most everyone was thoroughly drunk, including Ollie, for the first time in many years. Ake had passed out on the floor in a corner. Someone's wife was asleep in a chair. Kris, Nils, and Gunnar were standing on the stairs, laughing and singing songs that Ollie had a feeling were bawdy, but his Norwegian was so rough that he couldn't translate enough of the words to understand.

"Erik, I haven't had so much fun in years," Ollie told his friend in a slurred voice some time after midnight. "But I'm ready to collapse. Can you call me a cab to take me back to the hotel?"

"Nei, nei," his host replied. "I will drive you."

"Nei, nei," Ollie answered, "you are too drunk to drive."

"I'm a big man," Erik said, laughing. "I'm never too drunk to drive."

Several of the more sober guests tried to convince Erik that he should not drive, but to no avail. Erik rounded up Thor and Signe, who woke up Ake, while Ollie said his good-byes to the other Fishermen and their wives.

This time, Thor sat in the front passenger seat with Ake, who soon fell asleep again, on his lap. Signe and Ollie sat in back, Ollie pushing against the seat in front of him for security. Erik drove loosely, fluidly.

"Slow down for God's sake, slow down," Ollie yelled as the tires screeched when the car skidded around a sharp curve heading downhill with a steep hundred-foot drop on the right. "Why don't you just let Thor drive," Ollie asked as Thor reached over and held the steering wheel, helping Erik guide the car into its proper lane.

"I've known this road for more than fifty years," Erik said as he hunched over the steering wheel. "I could close my eyes and not miss a turn."

"But don't," Thor said, as Erik laughed.

When they arrived at the hotel Ollie kissed Signe on each cheek, shook hands with Thor, and patted the still sleeping Ake on his back.

"I'll pick you up for lunch," Thor told him before Erik pushed the seat up for Ollie to step out of the car. The two men hugged.

"Tomorrow night, my friend, we will make plans for fishing," Erik told him, grasping his arms and suddenly looking quite sober. "Rest up for our expedition."

Then Erik slapped his back, sat down in the car, and drove away before Ollie took his first staggering steps into the brightly lit hotel lobby.

Once inside his room, Ollie dialed his house, hoping to reach Polly. The phone rang four times until the answering machine message engaged. "You've reached the Larsen's," he heard Polly say. "You know what to do," and then there was a beep.

"Polly," he said, "pick up if you're there. Polly." He waited, wondering if she was outside gardening. Or meeting a friend for afternoon coffee. Maybe she was at the grocery store. "Just called to say good night," he said. "Good night." After he hung up, he realized he'd forgotten to tell her that he loved her.

He slipped off his shoes, turned off the light, and lay back on the double bed without bothering to brush his teeth or take off his clothes. He shut his eyes and tried to fall asleep, but he'd had so much to drink that he felt like he was back on the fishing boat at sea on that first day in the worst storm. He put one foot on the ground to steady himself, and soon he sank into the darkness of sleep, finally, more than a day and a half after his journey to Norway began.

...

The next day Ollie woke mid-morning, head foggy from drinking the night before. Sunlight haloed the four sides of the curtains. He rubbed his hands together to get the blood flowing then slowly bent and straightened his fingers, as he had to every morning to loosen the stiff joints. He got out of bed and opened the curtains, finding a crystal clear scene, the sea spreading out before his hotel room window for miles. It was a magnificent sight— tiny waves breaking in the distance, throwing spray into the air. The sun reflecting on the droplets made the sea look like a gigantic field of diamonds stretching as far as he could see. During his wartime stay in Bergen, Ollie's view of the area had been limited by the hideout's lone window, and the only time he climbed the seven hills surrounding the city was at night to set up or repair transmission towers. His existence had been like a rat's, hiding by day, scurrying around after dark.

He showered, and while he was packing his dirty clothes he came across a letter he'd found in his shoebox of war mementos: dog tags, the War Cross, the Freedom Cross, the Participation Medal, several letters from Erik and Thor, and the only letter he'd ever received from Kirsten, which included a small black and white photograph of herself. It was this letter that he'd hidden in the pocket of his suitcase before leaving San Francisco. He gently lifted the envelope and took out the letter, written on plain white paper that, with age, had turned brown at the edges. The letter was written in Norwegian, but even after all these years he could remember each line, word for word. How she'd married a Norwegian soldier who came from Kirkenes about a year after the war's end. But how, two years prior, she'd had a baby seven months after Ollie left the Pederson farm. How the child had not been strong. How the only doctor in the area had been taken away by the Germans at the beginning of the occupation and, without medical attention, the baby had died just a few weeks after birth. How the baby was Ollie's. How ever since the baby's death, she'd lived restlessly, unable to sleep soundly and given to dark days with guilt and sadness. How, finally, she thought that he should know about the child, that maybe by telling him she could find peace.

The old sadness returned as Ollie looked at Kirsten's delicate handwriting. He took several deep breaths as he placed the letter back in the envelope. The return address held Kirsten's married name and her address in Kirkenes. He had no idea if either piece of information was current, but it was all he knew about her.

The phone rang and before he answered it, Ollie folded the envelope and tucked it inside his wallet.

"*God dag,*" Thor said. "Are you still with us?"

"Barely," Ollie told him. "I'm on my way."

But first he tried calling Polly again. She answered the phone on the third ring.

"It's me," Ollie said.

"You're developing a habit of making middle of the night phone calls," she said softly.

"Sorry," he told her.

"I'm glad," she said. "How are you?"

"A little hung over and tired," he said. "And I miss you."

"You're safe though," she said.

He told her that he was. He reminded her that he would be staying at Erik's for the rest of his visit. He promised to call her with the number. And this time he remembered to tell her that he loved her before they hung up.

Thor was in the lobby, which was decorated with welcome banners and crowded with people checking in. Ollie vaguely recalled Erik mentioning something about the hotel being booked for some sort of dedication. Did Erik also say that they would be attending it? Ollie couldn't recall.

"You look none the worse for wear," Ollie told Thor.

"The secret is water," Thor said, taking Ollie's suitcase as they walked to the front desk. "A glass of water after every alcoholic drink."

"You should have told me this before the party last night," Ollie said.

"For the next time," Thor told him.

"The way I feel this morning, what next time?" Ollie said as they both laughed.

Ollie checked out of the hotel, and then he and Thor walked to Thor's car, an old blue Volvo sedan that was impeccably cared for, from washing and waxing the outside to conditioning the interior. Thor drove along the quay on the same route that Erik had taken them the day before, past the art galleries, restaurants, and boutiques. This time, however, Thor parked on the street, near the red-painted building where the hideout had been located. The familiar smell of the sea and of fish reminded Ollie of the hideout's straight-back chair where he sat surrounded by those odors for hours and hours while transmitting messages.

Thor and Ollie ate lunch—fried mackerel, herring burgers, potato dumplings, and stewed rhubarb—at the ground floor restaurant that Ollie learned a cousin of Thor's owned now. "I think my father was always a little disappointed that I didn't carry on his business, but I didn't know the first thing about food and I didn't care to learn," Thor said as they walked outside the restaurant and down the wood plank alleyway to the back. "My cousin is better suited to running a restaurant. He actually knows how to cook."

Thor started up the stairway to the museum. Ollie stood for a moment watching him. How many times had Ollie climbed up these steps, his ears thrumming with his heartbeats, believing that the Germans were watching him? That they would capture him? Or that they would simply shoot him, no questions asked? For the year that Ollie lived and worked in the hideout, every time he left the building he wasn't sure if he would make it back.

But here he was on a bright day in peacetime. Ollie took a deep breath, grabbed the rail, and walked up the stairs to the third floor landing.

"I come up here every now and then," Thor said. "Just to remind myself."

He opened the door and they entered the small outer room. There was the metal bed frame, the refrigerator, the stacked chairs, the cases of canned food, all as Ollie remembered, only everything was dusted as it hadn't been before. In the middle of the ceiling was a bare bulb that illuminated the space in a stark, harsh light. And across from Ollie and Thor stood the dresser, pulled back to reveal the hideout.

"It's like time has stopped here," Ollie told Thor as an older woman in a bright print dress walked from the hideout.

"*Hei* Mr. Erickson," the woman said. When she looked at Ollie she smiled and raised her arms as if she were readying to conduct a piece of music. "*Velkommen* Mr. Larsen," she said, shaking his hand. "I see your pictures every time I work. I feel I know you already."

"Mrs. Swanson is the museum's curator," Thor told Ollie.

"Come in, please," she said, leading them into the hideout.

The second room was just like the first, the same as it had been long ago. Below the dormer window facing Ollie were the two small beds that folded up against the wall to provide more space during the day while The Fishermen worked. Ollie remembered how soft and uncomfortable the mattresses were initially, although eventually he got used to the narrow beds with the weak springs. In front of the beds was the old wooden table with the wireless transmitter/receiver and headset that Ollie and the other men had used. Nearby, to the right, were two upholstered chairs, the leather seats cracked and torn, and behind them on the west wall was a pair of vintage submachine guns. In the corner was the tub in which he had bathed during the months he lived there. It had been too short, so Ollie had to squat in the tub and he remembered how cold it had been and how one of the things he longed for most during the war was a hot bath.

"It's amazing," Ollie said. "Just as it was."

"Some time after the war the men of the resistance raised money to open the museum," Thor told him.

"We interviewed many of The Fishermen to make the rooms look accurate," Mrs. Swanson said. "We get a lot of visitors who have never heard about the Norwegian underground."

"We had to stay silent about what we were doing for so long, it's like once we were free to speak, it felt wrong to say anything," Thor said.

"That's true," Ollie agreed, as he walked to the small window that looked out on the harbor. He had stood at that window hundreds, maybe thousands, of times, Ollie thought. Seeing the outside world, even just a framed portion of it, helped him from going stir crazy during his confinement in the hideout. He had watched the boats come in and out of the harbor. He followed people walking along the quay—fishermen on their way to their boats, women carrying sacks of groceries, children traveling to and from school. Sometimes he saw the German soldiers marching. Other times he watched the Gestapo halting people to search them, which made his heart rapid fire as he imagined his grandmother's sisters undergoing the same trauma and terror before they were taken away. Every now and then, when Ollie had seen a Nazi roughing up someone, he had been tempted to lift one of the submachine guns from the wall and shoot the German. But he never did so literally, knowing that he would only expose the resistance effort, knowing that The Fishermen's secret operations were the most effective means to shoot the Germans figuratively.

"Mrs. Swanson has collected some photographs, too," Thor said.

Ollie turned around to find the medicine cabinet, storage locker, icebox, stove, a small wood kitchen table, and three wooden chairs against the back wall along with a display of framed black and white pictures. He walked across the room and looked at the photos of the various Fishermen. Underneath each shot was a caption with the names and ages of the men, information about where they had gone to school, and who their parents were. In several cases the labels told the dates of the men's deaths. Ollie saw that three Fishermen died in German prison camps.

One photo in the center of the wall was larger than the others and featured Erik, Thor, and Evold, crowded together, squinting into the sun, all of them looking impossibly young and vigorous.

"The three of you were so big, you barely fit in the picture together," Ollie said.

"And you were so serious," Thor said, tapping the glass of the next photo with the caption, "*Olaf Larsen, Amerikansk, Helt.*"

"Hero," Thor said, pointing to the last word.

"I didn't feel like one," Ollie told him. "I certainly didn't look like one."

Ollie saw himself, radio headset on, staring at the wall of the hideout, a pencil in his hand. He must have been receiving a message. His forehead was furrowed, his lower lip pulled tight between his teeth. He had forgotten how he used to bite his lip, how he would get sores inside his mouth from chewing, how Valdy suggested he swish his mouth with salt dissolved in warm water to heal the self-inflicted wounds. Which worked until he gnawed at his lip again.

"I was always so nervous then," Ollie said, remembering the worry he felt about the messages being passed back and forth. One word improperly communicated could have resulted in Fishermen being captured and killed.

"I've often wondered what your life must have been like, all cooped up in this tiny room," Mrs. Swanson said, using her sleeve to wipe a smudge from the glass over a picture of Valdy. He stood tall on a pair of skis beside a giant pine tree, gazing at something in the distance, a faint smile on his lips. Below, the caption read, "*Valdemar Bjørn; overvært Holen Skole; sønn av Nils og Ingrid Bjørn; 1921-1943.*"

Reading the final date, Ollie inhaled sharply through his nose. His eyes stung with tears. Valdy had been his best friend during the war. He had helped to save Ollie's life, but Ollie hadn't been able to save Valdy. Soon after Ollie's escape over the border to Sweden, Valdy died. Only later, after the war, did Ollie learn the news from Erik, who wrote him with a bare bones report of the whereabouts of as many of The Fishermen as could be accounted for.

"I should have taken Valdy with me when we were in the mountains. Then he'd be alive today," Ollie said softly. He could hardly breathe, his throat thickening and his nose tingling.

Thor put his hand on Ollie's shoulder. "It wasn't your fault," Thor said. "You were both following orders, as you had to."

Ollie grasped his mouth with his hand, trying not to cry. But he did anyway, the sobs held inside him so that his stomach contracted and his back hunched over slightly, as if he were vomiting. Suddenly the smell of fish from the downstairs restaurant became overwhelming, the way the fish odor on the boat the first day of his assignment made him throw up. Ollie's face flushed and he felt lightheaded. He pushed past Thor to the hideout's doorway and the outer room, then made his way outside to the landing where he leaned against the railing, inhaling the salty air.

After awhile Thor joined him. "I couldn't stay long the first time, either," he said.

"The rooms are small but they hold so much," Ollie said.

The men walked down the steps and through the alley to the street. Thor began to unlock the door to his car.

"Could we keep walking?" Ollie asked. "I need some air."

"Absolutely," Thor said. "I've no plans the rest of the day."

"I'd like to see Rosenkrantz Tower," Ollie told him. "I never saw it close up while I was here."

"It wasn't like there was time for sightseeing during your last stay," Thor said.

"True," Ollie said as they began to walk. "Very true."

They traveled quietly for several blocks among groups of tourists, following the sidewalk along the quay, Ollie thinking about the hideout and the pictures of the men with whom he had served. "How is Ake?" Ollie finally asked. "He seems like a shell of himself, and it isn't just age."

"He suffers still from the torture," Thor said as they turned up the cobblestone walkway to the tower that had served as home for the Norse kings when Bergen was the country's capital. "Kraus broke Ake's hands with a hammer. He shocked him with cattle prods. He hung Ake from the walls just as he hung you. Ake's shoulders were pulled out of joint, his collarbone was broken. But he still wouldn't talk, so he was sent to Sachsenhausen, a concentration camp north of Berlin. Karl was taken there, too, and he died of tuberculosis. After the Germans were defeated, Ake came home. It was very sad. He'd lost more than forty pounds. His body was wrecked and his mind was badly damaged."

"God damn Kraus," Ollie said, stopping to lean against the old stone wall. He looked down at his own hands that Kraus had broken, too, the way over the years his fingers had started to twist slightly, right or left, like wind weathered tree limbs.

"We take care of him as best we can," Thor said, wiping at his forehead with a handkerchief. "He lives in a room off Eduard's fish warehouse. Ake feels at home with the smell of cod and salmon." He laughed softly and then said, "Kris has given him appliances and a TV. We all give him spending money and my cousin treats him to dinner at my father's old restaurant. Ake seems happy, although he often is in terrible pain. Despite everything, he keeps that wonderful, big smile on his face."

Ollie shook his head. "If you hadn't rescued me, I could have ended up like Ake," he said.

"No, my friend, Kraus would have killed you," Thor said. "Americans helping the underground took bullets to their foreheads."

Ollie knew it was true. Two days into his interrogation and torture, Kraus had held a gun to Ollie's head, threatening to kill him if he didn't provide the names of the underground members. The barrel was cold and prickly against Ollie's skin, strangely reminding Ollie of when he was a child in Minnesota and licked a metal pole in winter, his tongue sticking fast. But Ollie didn't speak. He was prepared to die. Only Kraus wasn't ready to let him just then. He wanted the information that Ollie could provide. So Kraus hung him on a wall by his wrists and began shocking him with an electric cattle prod.

"I've spent a lot of years trying not to think about Kraus, about any of this," Ollie told Thor, "or I would have gone crazy wondering why I lived when so many others died for no discernable reason."

Thor took him by the arm and walked him across the cobblestone courtyard, through a stone archway and onto a lawn, away from the tourists wandering the tower's grounds. "You must remember as much as you can about Kraus while you're here," he said quietly.

"What's this all about, Thor?" Ollie asked him.

"You need to be able to identify a certain variety of fish during our expedition," he said, adjusting his glasses.

Ollie thought of the cheesy "Goin' Fishin'" bumper stickers he'd seen on cars and trucks over the years. He had a feeling that this fishing trip was of a different sort. "Tell me the plan," he said.

"I can't here. You'll find out more tonight." Thor patted Ollie's shoulder.

"How long is this going to take, Thor?" Ollie asked. "There's a situation at work and I have to be back by Monday."

"You will," Thor said. "Come now," he told him as they began walking toward the looming tower, constructed in the 16th century of enormous stones, rough and weathered, but still standing.

OLLIE'S FIRST ORDER of business was interviewing The Fishermen to select the men he would train in assembling radio equipment and transmitting communications. He chose Karl for his aptitude at learning the code, Gunnar because he had taken some engineering courses at a local college and was good at construction, and Rolf since he had a sharp mind and a calm disposition, both necessary to send and receive messages.

It took Ollie three weeks to set up his small facility. The biggest problem was how to build a transmission tower on the roof without the Germans catching sight of it from the street or the surrounding mountains. Thor's father was the one who suggested disguising the tower as a laundry line on a small, flat portion of the roof where the restaurant's tablecloths, napkins, towels, and rags could be dried. One morning, on a rare day when rain wasn't expected, Thor, Karl, and Ollie climbed the steps to the roof, carrying wire, posts, and damp towels. The Nazi patrols hadn't started their rounds and the Germans weren't yet downstairs at the restaurant. The trio built the tower quickly, in twenty minutes, as they had practiced in the hideout for two days. They hung the towels on the line once they finished. Later that night, Rolf went up to the roof and removed the towels so that Ollie could send his first message in code to the British, several pre-selected lines from *Hamlet*: "For loan oft loses both itself and friend,/And borrowing dulls the edge of husbandry,/This above all: to thine own self be true."

Minutes later came the reply, "And it must follow, as the night the day,/Thou canst not then be false to any man."

"It worked," Erik shouted, clapping his hands.

"Quiet!" Thor whispered. "You'll get us all caught before we've done anything."

There was a routine to the short winter days, when sunlight appeared for only four hours, if at all, depending on the rain and the cloud cover. Teaching Karl, Gunnar, and Rolf in the morning. Tutoring Erik and Valdy in explosives later in the afternoon. Doing sets of sit-ups and push-ups to stay fit. And playing cards, dice, chess, or the Norse game of "tafl" during the off hours, when nothing was happening, which was most of the time at first. Sometimes Ollie felt he wasn't so much fighting a war as attending an odd overnight camp. He missed not hearing English spoken and sometimes tired of the effort it took to translate in his head what The Fishermen said, then think of a reply, and translate his response into Norwegian. Days passed without any communication activity, partly because the other towns with resistance members were still in the process of setting up their operations, and partly because if the operators spent too long on the radios it gave the German cryptographers more material to analyze and possibly decode. On clear days Thor or Rolf would return to the roof during the down time to hang damp tablecloths or napkins to dry on the line, keeping up the guise, ensuring that the Germans suspected nothing. For the same reason Erik and Evold took the boat out fishing for a few days each week to avoid suspicion. Ollie envied them. He wished that he were free to go outside, even for ten minutes, just to walk around the block and feel the rain in his hair, the cold surround his hands like a glove, and smell something other than fried fish from the restaurant below. But he couldn't chance being stopped by the Gestapo.

At the end of the second month, in January, a young boy dressed all in black appeared one evening. He had strawberry blond hair and his cheeks were red from running through the cold night.

"This is Kristian," Thor told Ollie. "One of our couriers."

"But he's a child," Ollie said.

"I'm already sixteen," the boy said, breathing hard. He leaned over to catch his breath before he reported that three German destroyers had been sighted hiding in a fjord at Alesund, to the north of Bergen. "Our contact said that they don't look as if they are ready to put out to sea any time soon. The ships have been camouflaged with tree branches," Kristian said.

Karl tapped out the communiqué, a coded line from Virgil—"Fortunate too is the man who has come to know the gods of the countryside."

Several nights later, Kristian returned while Erik, Ollie, Valdy, and Thor were playing cards. "A British sub planted explosives near the ships," he said. "One sunk, and the two others were badly damaged."

Before Erik could shout his approval, Thor put his hand over Erik's mouth. The others quietly shook hands with Kristian, and Valdy opened two bottles of warm beer from the storeroom to celebrate.

They later learned through their sources that the Gestapo had gone door to door in Alesund, asking questions of everyone, even small children, taking those they felt were suspicious away for further questioning about who was responsible for planting the explosives. A handful of men were sent to Ulven prison camp and had not been seen since. The Fishermen were warned to be extra careful about their activities and conversations, and especially of their contacts. The Nazis were trying to infiltrate the resistance movement. Trust no one, they were told.

For four long months Ollie stayed in the attic room, feeling as though he was doing little for the war effort other than watching the winter rain continue to fall, watching a leak in the ceiling close to the refrigerator grow from a yellow pinpoint to a large brown stain the shape of Wisconsin. A metal bucket caught the steady drips. During the times when Ollie had nothing to do the sound became irritating, like a continually barking dog.

"We've nothing to patch the roof with for now," Thor told him. "The Nazis have rationed everything."

Including sunshine, it seemed to Ollie. He came to understand why the Norwegians painted their buildings so brightly, the only promise he could see of brighter days ahead.

On a particularly rainy day, when water in the metal bucket had to be poured into the wash tub every half-hour because it filled so fast, Erik was arguing with Thor about the British government's strategies, or lack thereof, to defeat the Nazis. During a heated exchange between the two, Ollie received a radio message that additional equipment, explosives, and weapons for the underground would be dropped from an airplane over a farm a few miles north of Bergen near a small fjord in two days.

"Given the amount of supplies, I'll need seven other men for the retrieval mission," Ollie said as he turned around in his seat at the radio table and faced Valdy, who was sitting in one of the upholstered chairs and reading a book while Thor and Erik played chess at the kitchen table.

"What's this with 'I'll need'?" Erik asked, as Thor captured one of his pawns. "This is a mission for The Fishermen."

"And I'm going," Ollie said. Finally, he thought, he would have a chance to be a soldier again.

"No," Erik said, chuckling and shaking his head. "You are a radio specialist and need to stay with the radio."

Ollie bit at his cheek. "On orders from the SOE," he told Erik as he stood up, although why he wasn't sure. He knew he was no match for Erik. And, besides, he didn't want to fight him. They were supposed to be allies, fighting together against the Nazis. "I'm to signal the pilot, Erik," Ollie said.

"Any of us can manage that," Erik said, standing up as well.

"Not if Ollie's supposed to," Thor told him as he, too, pushed back his chair and stood.

"On whose authority?" Erik asked. "I'm not governed by the British."

"Stop, Erik," Valdy said, shutting his book as he looked from one man to the next.

"But he's not a Fisherman, as you'd know if you'd seen him on the boat," Erik said, pointing to Ollie.

Thor pressed the tips of his fingers against the edge of the table, restraining himself, Ollie thought. "He's more of a Fisherman than any of us," he said. "He's risking his life for a country that's not even his own."

Erik ran his hands through his thick red hair before sitting down again. He stared at the chessboard. "OK, so we'll take the four of us and Ake, Gunnar, Lars, and Evold," he said, as Ollie watched him move one of his castles, capturing Thor's remaining bishop.

Several days later, on a misty April day at dusk, Thor and Erik left the hideout carrying a case each of canned food that they took downstairs to the restaurant. Valdy stood watch at the outside door while Rolf and the boy, Kristian, looked out the dormer window and Ollie paced in the doorway to the hideout, waiting for Thor and Erik to give the all clear signal. He had not been outside in six months and he couldn't wait to get beyond the walls that had held him inside for so long. Yet the mission that he and the other Fishermen were about to embark on was the most dangerous assignment for any of them so far. The four men had spent the last two days contacting the other men who would be joining them, designing a plan to get everyone aboard Erik's boat without detection, plotting a course to and from the fjord where the boat would tie up, and making arrangements with Eduard, who owned the fish warehouse, to store the munitions until they could be distributed to the resistance members.

"Now," Valdy said, motioning for Ollie to follow him down the stairs.

"*Godt hell*," Rolf said.

"You too," Ollie said before Rolf and Kristian pulled the dresser shut against the wall.

Carrying a tin of cheeses, sausages, and bread, Ollie followed Valdy outside and down the wooden stairs. He could smell the salt from the sea. The cold air made his eyes water, and his heart began beating fast and strong in his ears with a nervousness for all that the men had to accomplish in the next day. Ollie and Valdy met Thor and Erik at the bottom of the steps.

"The Huns are thick inside but my father is offering a free round of beer right now, the cheapest variety that will make their heads ache tomorrow," Thor said before the men started down the wood-plank alley, past the restaurant's windows where they could hear the Germans talking loudly, glasses clinking, utensils scraping along plates.

Soon the four reached the Bryggen, cutting across the sidewalk along which businessmen were walking home from work. They crossed the wide cobblestone street to the Vaagen where they blended in with the other fishermen wearing similar sweaters, bibs, watch caps, rubber boots, smocks, and gloves. But those fishermen were unloading their catches for the day. Ollie's Fishermen were about to set off for a big catch of a completely different sort.

They boarded Erik's boat. "Are the fish running in Lofoten?" Erik asked, leaning over the ladder to the cabin.

"*Ja, ja,* they are," Ollie heard Evold reply to the coded greeting. Each of the four other men had gone aboard Erik's boat at different times of the day to hide in the berth.

"Good, good," Erik said as Ollie and Valdy went below immediately, as planned, because too many men visible on deck would call attention to the vessel as it set out to sea.

In the cabin, Ollie found Gunnar making coffee, Ake napping on a bunk, and Evold sitting at the table playing cards with a thin young man with brown eyes the color of tree bark. Each man had a small pile of dried lentils near his hands.

"*Velkommen,*" Gunnar said.

"*Til slutt,*" Evold said, setting down his cards before nudging Ake's leg. Ake snorted as he woke. "You take my place, and my lentils," Evold told Ollie as the young man stood and held his hand out.

"You are Olaf, I think," he said as Ollie shook his hand. "I'm Lars."

"One of our finest skiers," said Valdy.

"Good to meet you," Ollie said, sitting down in Evold's chair. Gunnar brought him coffee.

"Watch out for Olaf," Ake said as he started climbing the ladder. "He's a cardsharp." He laughed as he left the cabin with Evold.

Ollie, Valdy, Gunnar, and Lars sat around the small table playing poker as the boat sailed out of the harbor, a Norwegian fishing vessel like any other. At least that was what Ollie and the rest of the men had to remember. If they were stopped, Ollie and Valdy would have to hide beneath the bunks so that the crew size seemed reasonable. The others were to say that they were on their way north to Lofoten where they'd heard the herring were running well. Ollie had discovered that so much of war was deception that it was hard for him sometimes to remember what was real, which was why he kept losing, hand after hand, at poker. He tried to concentrate on the cards he was dealt but his focus wasn't on what was just in front of him. Rather his attention was above, to what he imagined was out beyond the breakwater. German snipers positioned along the coast. War planes flying low through the air. Nazi boats patrolling the waters.

An hour and a half into the trip, with the fishing boat moving smoothly through the water, Ollie pushed his half dozen remaining lentils to Lars after losing again. Valdy said, "If we had money to bet, Lars would be the big winner."

"And Olaf would owe us many drinks," Gunnar added before he gave Ollie a new supply of beans from his cache.

"*Mange takk*," Ollie said. "I'll pay up after the war."

Ollie felt the boat turning, and soon Thor came below and told them, "Evold sighted the buoy. Ready yourselves."

The men set down their cards before taking off their fishing garb. Underneath the bibs and braces, the flannel shirts, and thick woven sweaters, they wore black or blue turtlenecks or sweaters and dark pants. Gunnar was in his Sunday dress slacks, Valdy had a pair of ski pants—whatever dark clothing the men had been able to find at their homes, they wore. Ollie's was a British issued commando turtleneck and pants uniform, and one pocket held a signal mirror and a field torch. On his wrist he wore a watch synchronized to Greenwich mean time, an hour ahead of the Norwegian time zone.

One by one the four men above came below to change their clothes, putting back on their rubber fishing boots once they finished. They stashed their fishermen clothing beneath the thin bunk mattresses. Each put on black watch caps, pulled tight over the head, covering the hair, and fetched their sacks and tins of food. Before going above, Valdy opened the footlocker where two rifles, a submachine gun, and a half-dozen grenades were stored beneath the rain poncho and dark blue sweater that Ollie wore during his first journey on the boat. Valdy tossed Ollie the sweater.

"You'll need this too," he said as Ollie slipped the sweater over his head.

Then Lars took one rifle, Gunnar the other, Valdy slung the strap of the submachine gun over his shoulder, and Ollie clipped grenades to their belts and his own.

Once on deck, Ollie had to blink his eyes to adjust his vision to the darkness of the cove that Evold was steering the boat through. The boat's motor echoed against the surrounding cliffs. The only illumination came from the boat's running lights. The sky was cloudy and a misty rain fell. Ollie could barely make out the forms of the other men in their black clothing, silhouettes hunkering around the wheelhouse. He followed Lars.

"Not getting sick are you?" Erik asked as Ollie passed him.

"Hush," Thor said.

Lars and Ollie hurried to the bow where Gunnar and Valdy were already posted, looking and listening not only for signs of spying eyes, but for their contact as well. Evold cut the motor, the boat drifting, water sloshing against the sides.

After a few minutes Ollie said, "Look there," pointing starboard to Evold.

A small light swung seemingly by itself in the night. Evold started the engine again and motored slowly toward a short dock sheltered by tall trees whose branches hung over the water, secluding the landing. There a young boy stood with a kerosene lantern in one hand. He looked to be only ten or eleven.

As the boat neared, Erik shouted to him, "Are the fish running in Lofoten?"

"Ja, ja, they are," the boy replied.

"So young," Ollie said to Valdy.

"His father was a Norwegian soldier sent north last year to Falstad prison camp by the Nazis," Valdy explained. "His grandfather hates the Germans and helps us any way he can."

Lars threw the boy the bowline, which he used to tie up the boat next to a dinghy at the dock. The men disembarked, as quickly and as quietly as they could, following the child to the start of a narrow dirt path that cut through evergreen trees.

"Can you lead us without the light?" Thor asked. "Otherwise we're easy marks."

"Ja," the boy said. "I know this trail since I can walk."

"We'll line up then," Valdy said. "Alternate between those who have weapons and those who don't."

Lars was first behind the boy followed by Ake, Ollie, Evold, Gunnar, Thor, Erik, and Valdy at the rear. They each placed a hand on the shoulder of the man in front.

"Ready?" the child asked.

"OK," Valdy said before the boy put out the lantern.

Ollie could see nothing, as if his eyes were shut. He felt Ake begin walking and he did the same, taking one small step after another. The men moved silently, like a caterpillar, inching their way through the dark, wet forest guided by the boy and his memory of the trail. Ollie stepped on the back of Ake's boots several times. Evold bumped Ollie once when the procession slowed. By the time they reached a field, the rain was coming down cold and hard and the dirt path that skirted the pasture was a trough of mud. Ollie felt the soles of his boots clumping with the muck, and he was breathing hard from the hike. He'd been shut away in the hideout for so long.

Behind him, Ollie heard Gunnar curse, "*Forbann det*. Hold up, hold up." Evold stumbled into Ollie, who bumped Ake.

"What's going on?" Lars asked as the line came to a stop.

"My boot stuck in the mud and my foot pulled free. I can't find my boot," Gunnar said.

"I have it," Ollie heard Thor say.

"Jesus, hurry it up before we're soaked clear through," Erik told them.

"I'm trying, *forbann det*," Gunnar said again.

"Shush. There are small ears in our midst," Valdy said before the line began slowly moving once more, around the field and up a slight hill to a white farmhouse with a candle burning in one window.

"Stay here," the boy said, leaving the men standing at the side of the house as he ran to a barn. Ollie could hear him knocking on the door, which was soon opened. A soft yellow light spilled out over the boy, who motioned for the men to join him.

They hurried to the barn where an older, humped man holding a lantern waited in the doorway.

"*Hei*, Kåre," Valdy said.

"*Velkommen*," the man told the men, nodding at each one. He brought them, muddy and cold, inside the small barn that was crowded with bales of hay, farming tools, and a cow in each of the two stalls. "There's quilts to keep you warm," the man said, pointing to a corner where a half dozen blankets were stacked. "I wish I could offer you better accommodations."

"You've given the supplies a safe place to land," Valdy said. "What more can we ask of you, Kåre?"

The man and boy told The Fishermen good night before they walked back to the farmhouse, leaving the lantern with Valdy. As Evold wrapped himself in a blanket, Ake petted a cow, and the other men ate from their tins and sacks, Ollie walked over to the corner where the tools were stored. Among a rusty collection of spading forks, scoops, pitchforks, rakes, and pick axes, Ollie found a round point shovel with a wooden handle split down the middle with age and held together with baling wire wrapped around the wood.

"It's the best we have," Ollie told Gunnar, handing him the shovel. "The trench should be dug at the edge of the woods. I'd make it long rather than deep." He reached into his pocket and pulled out the torch. "Use this to find your way," he said, handing the flashlight to Lars.

"There are eyes in those woods, though, I'm sure of it," Thor said as he chewed his cheese and bread. "So use that only if you absolutely need the light."

"And keep your boots on," Erik told Gunnar, who said a word in reply that Ollie hadn't learned in his Norwegian language class. Erik laughed in response.

Ollie and Ake agreed to take first watch and were given the submachine gun and one of the rifles to use at their post. Ollie unhooked the grenades from his belt and distributed them to the men inside. Then Gunnar and Lars, still armed with the other rifle, left the barn with Ollie and Ake.

Outside the rain continued to fall, like drops of mercury through the night sky.

"*Godt hell*," Ake told Lars and Gunnar as the two started back to the forest.

Ollie and Ake stood outside the barn, pacing beneath the eave, watching the rain fall, listening for voices or footsteps. But the only activity they witnessed was Gunnar and Lars, wet and even muddier, returning to relieve them after digging the trench.

"Thor and Erik are on next," Ollie said as Lars handed him the field torch and Ollie gave them his wristwatch. Then Ollie and Ake went back inside the barn to rest. Ollie never really slept, though. The ground was cold and hard, Ake snored, Erik shouted in his sleep, Evold kept sneezing, and in his mind Ollie continued to run over the logistics for the next phase of their mission. Whenever he started drifting to sleep, he'd jerk awake, uneasy about what awaited him in the morning when he was to signal the pilot with the mirror that was tucked in his pocket. So he listened to cows restless in their stalls and to the water dripping through the roof. He turned one way. Then another. And the other way again. For hours. Finally, when Evold and Valdy came inside the barn to fetch him, he was sitting against the wall, eating the rest of the cheese in his tin. Valdy gave him back the wristwatch while Lars woke Ake.

"Soon, *ja?*" Valdy asked Ollie.

"Wake the others and have them ready to go," Ollie told him.

Ollie and Ake returned outside with a rifle and the submachine gun. It was just after six o'clock in the morning, Greenwich mean time, and a diffused light outlined the shapes around them but provided no definition or detail. In addition to watching for the enemy on this post, Ollie and Ake were to listen for the British Halifax carrying the supplies that were due to arrive sometime before seven. Ollie felt jittery from the lack of sleep and his eyes burned as he stared out at the farmhouse and the field below. The sight was postcard perfect, but not ideal for their mission. The rain had finally stopped, leaving a mist that shrouded the air and the ground like a bride's lace veil. Without sunlight, Ollie would have to use the field torch to reflect the signal. He reached into his pocket and took out the mirror and the flashlight.

"Do you hear something?" Ake asked, pointing to the sky behind them.

Ollie turned around, facing the barn and the woods to the rear, listening to the men waking inside, whispering to each other, and also to what sounded like a low clucking and hooting coming from the trees. "Chickens?" he asked.

"Not the ptarmigans," Ake said. "Listen again."

Ollie shut his eyes, concentrating. There was a deep drone in the distance, like ocean waves, that grew louder. He looked at his watch. It was almost six-thirty. "Cover me," Ollie told Ake before Ollie ran to the side of the farmhouse. He turned on the flashlight and held it above the mirror, tilting the mirror up and down, up and down continuously. This was the part of the plan that had weighed on him all night. He wouldn't know until the last moment whether the plane he was signaling was the Halifax or one of the Nazi single-prop Stukas, the dive bombers with whistling wing sirens that had attacked London mercilessly in 1940. He wasn't a religious man, but as he waited he prayed, just in case, to whomever or whatever, that he wasn't signaling death on himself, The Fishermen, and the farmer and his family.

Suddenly the plane was skimming the tops of the tall pine trees in front of him. Ollie counted the four props of the Halifax as the plane passed over him, engines screaming. He turned and watched as the plane dropped the six-crate load, rectangular and square and unmarked, buoyed on white parachutes that floated down slowly, like dandelion fluff, landing perfectly in the field without catching in the surrounding trees.

"Now," Ollie shouted to Ake, who opened the barn door. The Fishermen streamed outside as the plane banked sharply to the left and climbed rapidly into the fog as it headed over the North Sea, back toward its base in northern England.

The men ran into the muddy field, Lars and Valdy leading the way, with Thor, Ollie, and Ake fanning out behind the others to provide cover with their weapons. Evold and Erik pulled the parachutes from the crates and bundled them up together for Lars and Gunnar to drag into the woods and bury in the trench that they dug the night before. Meanwhile, Evold and Ollie went ahead with the submachine gun and rifle to scout the path to the boat, making sure the way was clear for Erik, Thor, Valdy, Ake, Lars, and Gunnar to carry the crates.

As Ollie was stepping onto the path from the field, he slipped, falling on his back. He managed to keep the rifle pointed up and his finger off the trigger. The mud quickly seeped through his pants and sweater.

"Here," Evold said, offering Ollie his hand and helping to pull him back onto his feet. Evold sneezed twice. "You've just become acquainted with our muck season the hard way." He wiped his nose with his sleeve.

"I'm afraid so," Ollie said as the mud dripped down his back and legs inside his clothes and boots.

He and Evold began slowly walking along the path, looking left then right through the immense trees. Ollie saw Lars covering up the trench with dirt and Gunnar spreading handfuls of dead pine needles over the ground. Behind him, the other Fisherman carried the supplies on their shoulders as they trudged through the field. Ake held a long, rectangular crate on each shoulder.

"Look at Ake," Ollie whispered.

"He is like an ant," Evold said. "He can carry many times his body weight."

They plodded on as quietly as they could, watching and listening for signs of danger. The only sounds were the trees creaking in the wind and one lone bird—a grouse, Evold thought—that flapped its wings in anger at being disturbed, as well as several frogs calling. Occasionally a breeze blew through the pines, sprinkling water from the needles onto their heads. They listened but did not speak in case there were German patrols in the woods.

About halfway through the forest, Ollie and Evold pulled up. They held their hands out toward the other Fishermen, who stopped walking as well. The men looked up through the trees, past the canopy of branches to the sky, listening to the whir of an approaching plane.

"It couldn't be one of ours," Erik said to Ollie with a wry laugh. "As you may have noticed, Norway has no airforce."

"Don't move," Thor whispered. "Stay as still as possible."

But even with the warning, Evold sneezed, Ake shifted from side to side under the weight of the crates, and Gunnar coughed, trying to catch his breath.

Ollie saw the dark form of the plane pass over them and for a moment he imagined himself as a field mouse watching a bird of prey circle, feeling helplessly visible and completely without options.

"What if they see the boat?" Ollie asked Erik.

"Hopefully they'll think she belongs to someone who lives nearby. The important thing is they don't see us," he told Ollie.

They waited ten minutes, in case the plane doubled back. But it did not, the buzz of the engine fading as the plane continued northward. They resumed their cautious trek, arriving at the boat a half-hour later.

The men left the crates at the edge of the woods and boarded the boat to bring wooden fish barrels up from the berth. Erik carried two crow bars, one of which he gave to Thor and the two men pried open the crates in the seclusion of the trees. The other men quickly unloaded the cargo—guns, grenades, dynamite, and ammunition—into the barrels that they returned to the boat, below deck. Ollie and Lars stashed the planks from the crates under fallen trees, beneath pine needle mounds, behind the craggy shore-line rocks. By the time all the barrels were stowed and the men had changed out of their wet clothes to their fishing garb again, it was close to nine in the morning.

"A good day for fishing," Erik said once they finished. "We'll fill the hold and go home."

Evold sneezed again. "Get dry, get some sleep, and get well," he said as Lars untied the boat from its mooring.

Ollie went below with Thor, Ake, and Valdy as Evold steered the boat from the dock, through the fjord at two-thirds speed. Thor set about to make a pot of coffee, Valdy stored the weapons in the footlocker, and Ake lay down on a bunk. Ollie took off his muddy boots and stripped off his wet sweater, hanging it on a peg, then he lay down on the other bed. This time Ollie was able to sleep, heavily and deeply, until he felt his shoulder being jostled and heard a high-pitched voice saying, "Up, up," in English.

He couldn't remember where he was or even what year it was. He expected to see his childhood room and find his mother trying to wake him for school until he opened his eyes and saw Ake. "Hurry, hurry!" Ake said, pointing below the bunks.

"What?" Ollie asked.

"There's a boat nearby," Thor said. "You must hide."

Ollie scrambled from the bunk and crawled beneath it, curling up his legs so that his feet didn't stick out, which reminded him of when he played hide-and-seek as a kid. This time, however, the stakes were higher. Ake scrambled under his bunk and Thor made up both, pulling the blankets down low on the sides and the foot ends of the bunks. Ollie felt the boat slow to a stop and rock in its own wake.

Thor told them, "Valdy and I are going above. If it's not right, I'll come back down and do my best to keep you from being found."

Then Ollie heard Thor and Valdy climb the rungs to the deck.

Meanwhile Erik's voice was booming a greeting to someone. He sounded relaxed, more relaxed than he'd be with a German patrol. At least that's what Ollie hoped.

"What's up, you old pirate?" an unfamiliar voice said from the deck.

"Any luck, Nils?" Erik shouted.

"Must be Nils Anderson," Ake said to Ollie. "He has the *Mermaid*."

"How could we have fish when we just left the harbor, Erik?" the man, Nils, asked. "Your hold is empty, too."

"We're heading to Lofoten. We hear the fish are starting to run there," Erik said.

"It's about time. They're late this year," Nils answered. "Probably all those damn German ships have the herring nervous, too." And then his voice dropped low, too low for Ollie to make out what Nils was saying. He continued to listen as Erik and Nils' conversation turned to a murmur.

After a few minutes, Ollie heard Erik say, "*Silk lang*," and the boat's engine was restarted. As the boat began to motor through the water, Ollie heard Thor return below and say, "All clear, at least for now."

Ollie and Ake crawled out from under the bunks, Ollie bumping his head on the frame. He sat down on the bunk and rubbed his head. Valdy and Erik joined the three in the berth. Erik's face was redder than usual and he paced back and forth. Valdy sat down in one of the chairs and held his face in his hands.

"It was Nils, yes?" Ake asked.

"Ja," Thor told him. "He put out to sea early today in case the Germans decide to close the port again. He said there's been trouble up north, in Telavåg. Two members of the resistance shot and killed a Gestapo officer. So the Nazis burned the town yesterday and sent everyone away to camps."

"Everyone?" Ake asked, shaking his head.

"Everyone," Thor said, taking off his glasses and wiping his eyes.

"My God," Ollie said quietly. He tried to imagine the same thing happening to the small town in Minnesota where he grew up, but he couldn't. It was an unthinkable thought made real.

"Sons of bitches," Erik said, banging his hand on the small table.

"Nils says there's word that the Germans are planning to go door-to-door in other towns where there's been resistance activity. Like Bergen," Thor told Ollie and Ake.

"Then it's too dangerous for us to return now," Valdy said.

"Especially with him along," Erik said, pointing at Ollie. "I knew we shouldn't have brought him."

"He's the reason we have these supplies in the first place," Thor said.

Erik jammed his hands into his pockets and began pacing again. After a moment Valdy said, "Lars and I can stay with Ollie on Holsnoy Island. It's not far and we have the safe house. We can ride out the troubles there."

"That's not a bad idea," Thor said.

"But you don't have to stay with me. You've risked enough already," Ollie said, still thinking about Telavåg and what the Germans would do to those who collaborated with people like Ollie. "I've been through survival training with the Brits. I can go it alone."

"No, no. Lars and I set up the cabin six months ago. We know the island, we know where the rations are hidden," Valdy said. "The rest of The Fisherman can take a few days to fish and fill the hold before returning to Bergen. Then they'll pick us up once the danger has passed."

Ake nodded his head. Thor said, "Yes."

"It's settled," Erik said, turning to climb the rungs to go above.

"All right then," Ollie said, although he realized that Erik wasn't looking for his concurrence.

Evold set a course that gradually drew the boat into the open sea. Time passed slowly as the men took turns watching for other boats that could be German patrols. And it was Lars who saw the rapidly moving craft first. Right away the men knew that the vessel was German, what with its heavy machine gun on the bow.

"Ollie and Valdy," Thor said, not even having to explain any further what the two men should do. They went below quickly, hiding under the bunks. Ollie heard German spoken loudly through a bullhorn and felt a heavy bump as the German boat came alongside.

The vibration of the motor through the floor ceased as Evold cut the engine. Ollie found himself shaking, as if he were cold. He gripped his hands together and closed his eyes, listening to footsteps as the Germans boarded the fishing boat.

"Let me see your papers," an officer demanded curtly.

Ollie heard Erik reply, "Ja, ja," with a forced laugh.

There was a long silence.

"What is your business out here?" the officer asked.

"We've been trying to fish but have been slowed by engine trouble and haven't caught anything much yet," Erik said. "We'll give you what we've already landed, if you wish," he offered.

A different officer said, "Ja, fresh herring or cod would taste good. We are coming in from two weeks on sea duty and we have had no fresh food for several days. Ja, we would like that."

"Ake, go below and bring some fish up for the sailors," Erik shouted.

Ollie heard Ake descending the stairs to the hold, whistling nervously. Ollie held his breath listening for the Germans to come below as well but no one did.

"Have you seen anything suspicious? Any English ships?" one of the Germans asked Erik while Ake knocked a pail several times against the table, making noise as if he were working hard to gather up all the fish they didn't have.

"Nei, nei." Erik said as Ake climbed above. "No other boats."

"Here," Ollie heard Ake say.

"Tomorrow we head up to Lofoten where the fish are running, I think," Erik said.

One of the Germans laughed. "Then you can give us more fish later," he said.

Ollie heard the fishermen laughing stiffly. "Ja, ja," Erik said.

Another said, "You should be careful out here. There are islands beyond with dangerous rocks offshore."

"Ja," Erik said. "Good advice. Takk."

There was a shuffling of footsteps and then Ollie heard Evold start the engine.

"Are they gone?" Valdy asked.

"I hope so," Ollie said.

But the two men waited without moving until Erik and Ake came below and told them that they could come out again.

"God, I was scared," Ollie said as he stretched his cramped legs.

"We all were," Erik said.

"Especially when I had to give them the fish," Ake said. "I thought the Germans would shoot me because I gave them old fish we should have thrown overboard for bait. But they didn't know the difference." He broke into peals of joyful laughter, jumping up and down on his short legs and holding his stomach as though he was sick.

...

It was nearly dark when Evold slowly piloted the boat into a small rocky cove surrounded by large trees. A low hill rose gently about one hundred yards behind the shore and provided some shelter from possible prying eyes to the west. The Fishermen had chosen the place carefully. Passing ships could not see the small beach or boats that were landing, and the cabin was well hidden from all sides.

They dropped anchor and watched the shore for a long time, searching for signs of life. Finally when they were convinced no one was within sight or sound, Valdy announced it was time to go. Ollie, Lars and Valdy climbed into the fishing boat's dinghy and Lars rowed them quickly to shore.

They carried two rifles, an ax, blankets and the food remaining from their tins. It was a bare minimum of the necessities for three men, but there were more blankets and food hidden in the cabin. Their friends on the fishing boat also would need food for the next few days while they fished and would not be able to forage on shore, so food supplies had been carefully divided.

After they landed, they waved to the crew on the boat and ran to the shadowy protection of the woods. Valdy slowly circled the cabin to check that no one had been there recently. Holding the ax, he carefully opened the door. Ollie and Lars covered him with their rifles.

A few moments later he waved them in. He reported that their emergency supplies had not been touched. Then he told them he would signal the fishing boat that all was well, that The Fishermen could leave.

The cabin was sturdily built, a place used by hunters. There were cobwebs and animal droppings everywhere. In addition to the animal mess and dirt, the cabin contained two wooden beds, a fireplace, table and three wooden chairs. At home, Ollie thought, it would be considered rustic if not dilapidated, but it was functional for a few days and suited their purpose.

While there still was a little light they set about collecting firewood. Although the fire could not be lit during the short daylight hours when smoke might be seen by enemy eyes, it would be needed at night for cooking and warmth. They chopped lush pine boughs to serve as mattresses.

When he had first inspected the cabin Valdy had moved some old logs that covered loose boards. They re-covered the trap door where the supplies, including a long hunting knife, had been cached beneath the floor. At first glance the cache had appeared to be intact. On closer inspection, however, they discovered some of the food had spoiled, including some rice, salted meat, and apples. This meant that they would be on even shorter rations if they had to stay longer than a few days, unless they could forage successfully in the woods.

"We must go out hunting tomorrow," Valdy said authoritatively. "Erik may not return for a few days and we will be very hungry, but there are deer on the island."

"Ja," Lars answered soberly. "But we both are good shots and maybe also there are rabbits or other game."

"Are you a good shot, Ollie?" Valdy asked.

"Not great, but okay," he replied modestly although he had won several

National Rifle Association medals in high school. "I had a lot of training in the special camp, and I used to hunt with my father back home, so I think I can hit a squirrel from a hundred feet or so if necessary." Ollie wondered how good his companions were.

Ollie knew that the Gulf Stream kept the Bergen region relatively warm in winter and that it was an area of heavy rainfall. Rarely was there much snow. That night, however, a blizzard began to howl and a heavy snow fell. By morning the strong wind had piled snowdrifts against the snug cabin, making it impossible to go out to search for food or scout for possible dangers.

Snow continued to fall all day and through the next night. To pass the time the three men told stories, described their homes and families, discussed the war and planned how to increase the food supply once the storm abated and they could go outside.

They agreed the first order of business would be to scout for several miles in each direction to be certain that there were no Germans nearby. If it was safe, they could hunt in the woods, where rifle shots would be muffled by the thick stands of trees.

The storm eased a little the next day, although snow still was falling in the morning and they were forced to remain inside. That afternoon, before it grew dark, they managed to push the door open enough so that they could exit. Then they began scouting, slogging through the wet snow. Valdy climbed a low hill behind the cabin from which he could get a good view to the west. Lars headed south along the line of trees, while Ollie, alone and strangely exhilarated, walked north through the edge of the trees so that tracks could not be seen from the shore or air.

Ollie made slow time, covering only a few miles and seeing only trees, very white glaring snow, and the shoreline. A little edge of the cove was visible as well. He felt alone in the bleak landscape, almost as if he was the only person on earth, and he felt nervous. But at least there were no signs of Germans.

When they finally rendezvoused, no one had seen signs of life nearby. Nevertheless it was decided they would take turns as lookouts during daylight hours.

The next morning, however, it was snowing hard again and a cold wind from the north dropped the temperature well below freezing. Further scouting, lookout duty and hunting were impossible. They did not have extra clothing and there was nothing to be gained by venturing out in the storm and getting wet.

Several books and old Norwegian magazines had been hidden with the food and blankets and the three men tried to read with the aid of a kerosene lamp and what little daylight filtered through a single window. But by mid-afternoon they gave up reading, deciding to rest their eyes and hoard their meager supply of kerosene for evenings and emergencies.

Their most promising find was a water-stained deck of cards hidden in a drawer of the single old table. After the cards were carefully pried apart they helped to relieve boredom for a while, but none of them were enthusiastic card players. The evening was spent taking turns telling about their lives when they were boys, discussing world politics, and plotting strategy for a possible Allied invasion of Norway for which they could only hope.

Valdy told about his experience training for the Olympics and winning the Norwegian cross-country skiing championship. He said that he had a cousin who had worked for the government but had disappeared when the Germans marched in. "No one in our family knows whether or not he is alive, in prison or hiding with a resistance group," he said bitterly. "I do not get angry easily, but I hate what those people are doing to our people and our country. 'Master race,' shit. They are psychopaths, you know?"

Lars held his hands against his head for a few moments before responding. "I think everyone in Norway has a story or a reason to hate the Nazis," he said. "A neighbor I grew up with, my best friend, was Jewish. A few nights after the Germans had come to Bergen the Gestapo agents broke into his house and took the whole family away. We have not seen or heard from my friend or his wife or their children. We have all heard stories about the concentration camps, and we can only assume that my friends were shipped to one of them." As he told the story he strode back and forth across the small cabin.

He was a tall thin man with high cheekbones and large brown eyes. Lars had been a middle distance runner on the college track team and he had kept in shape even though there were no track meets anymore. He had told Ollie that he was studying electrical engineering at the university.

Lars cleared his throat several times before he could speak again. "I saw German soldiers march down Kong Oscarsgate and bump right into two old ladies who had been shopping. They knocked the ladies down and laughed. I wanted to kill them."

Ollie listened to his companions and then told about his own great aunts having been taken away. He said that Americans did not know what was going on, and stories like they had told were not in American newspapers. "Some day the truth will come out, and then my people will get mad. We do not like injustice."

"America better wake up soon or it may be too late for freedom," Valdy responded with more than a touch of bitterness.

When they awoke on the fifth morning the snowfall had eased up, but a harsh gale wind was rushing across the island, whipping loose snow into the air. Walking under these conditions in sub-freezing weather would have been difficult if not impossible. Toward noon, however, they were able to trudge to the shore where they could see that turbulent waves would keep small boats within the safety of their home harbors. Erik would be unable to rescue them for at least another day.

As darkness began to fall, the temperature warmed slightly and the wind calmed, so they went out to forage for more wood near the cabin. Hunting and fishing, however, were still out of the question and the three men began to worry about their food supplies. They carefully measured out the rice that had not spoiled. It was divided into piles for another three days, by which time they hoped to be rescued. Then they cut up some sausage and cheese that they had brought from the boat and divided it into small but equal portions. In addition there were several loaves of stale bread that Gunnar had given them from the galley.

The next morning was cloudy and cold but the storm had moved out. Heavy snowdrifts still forced them to stay close to the cabin. Valdy decided they should get exercise to keep in shape, and they fashioned primitive snow shovels out of old boards found near the cabin. It took the rest of the afternoon using their knives and the ax to make two sets of flimsy snowshoes. Cutting and tying strips of old cloth they made bindings, but the cloth was too weak to hold their feet to one set of snowshoes and broke when Valdy started to walk. The other set was serviceable, however, and on the morning of the seventh day Valdy climbed the hill awkwardly and carefully, with a rifle strapped to his back and the hunting knife hanging from his belt, and soon disappeared into the woods on the other side of the hill.

Ollie watched his friend striding away, or as near to striding as could be done with the awkward snowshoes. Valdy stood out against the snow with his blond hair blowing in the wind. It was a dramatic sight, but Ollie worried about whether Valdy could find game and whether he could survive alone out in the cold, wet air with the wind whistling angrily.

He was gone for almost four hours and Ollie and Lars began to worry that he had had an accident. "Should we go out and try to track him?" Lars asked uncertainly, looking out the little window while Ollie paced back and forth in the small cabin.

"Hell, we should not have let him go out alone in this weather," he said to Lars almost accusingly.

"You're right, Ollie, but you know Valdy. He feels responsible for us and he wanted to find food."

Finally, when the darkness was complete, Valdy appeared, hauling part of a deer he had shot. He had skinned and quartered the carcass with the hunting knife. Then he had dragged part of the meat several miles through the snow, leaving most of the carcass cached in a tree to be collected the next day. After catching his breath he said, "As I started back the cloth binding broke and I had to abandon the second pair of snowshoes."

The sea outside their cove remained rough. On the morning of day eight, they agreed they probably would be stranded for at least another day or two before a boat could get to them.

But it was an optimistic hope. Except for the storm, the first week had been uneventful. They still had a little food, supplemented by Valdy's deer, and the cabin was reasonably warm. In fact the worst problem, other than no one coming back for them, had been boredom.

On the twelfth day, however, Lars hiked north along the edge of the woods on the daily scouting routine. About an hour later he returned, running to the cabin as if he were in a race. "There's a boat anchored in the next cove," he reported breathlessly, "about forty feet long with a machine gun mounted on the bow. It's flying a German flag."

"Did you see anyone on shore?" Valdy asked sharply.

"No, but there's a small lifeboat tied up to a tree. It looks like some of the Germans may have come ashore." Lars gasped for breath.

"How many do you think there are?" Ollie asked.

"From the footprints, one or two," Lars said.

"We better take to the woods fast and make the cabin look deserted," Ollie said nervously.

"I agree," Valdy said, "although I don't think we have to rush. It will be more important not to leave any clues, so we must clean up the cabin immediately in case we must leave on a minute's notice."

"Lars, go back and watch them," Ollie said. "Stay in the woods and if more land and head this way, come back fast, but stay hidden in the woods. We don't want them to see your tracks leading to the cabin. Valdy, let's start hiding what we can under the floor. I'll take the ashes from the fireplace and hide them up the hill."

Using an old board as a shovel, Ollie put the ashes into a broken bucket and climbed the hill until he found a good hiding place between two huge boulders with a cover of thick bushes between them. There he dumped the ashes and ran back through the woods to the cabin.

Meanwhile Valdy hid their food and camouflaged the loose boards by covering them with the old logs. The two men stashed the rest of the supplies in their blankets. As they finished the job Lars emerged from the woods.

"I saw three men rowing to shore and I ran back as fast as I could," he told them breathlessly.

"It's time to get out," Valdy announced calmly.

They carried their supplies up to the hiding place where Ollie had dumped the ashes.

"If we have to fight this is a good spot for an ambush," Ollie said. "They won't be able to see us and the rocks will give us protection, but fighting is our last resort. They'll have more fire power and they can wait us out, so our best defense is to stay hidden. Lars and I will watch in both directions from here where we have a good view. Valdy, find a place where you can see the shore and their boat, and warn us if the shore party finds the cabin. Remember, we don't shoot unless they find us. But if you have to shoot don't aim for the head. I learned in training that it's too easy to miss. Aim for the stomach. That's the best target." For the first time since meeting The Fishermen, Ollie was acting as a leader and he felt proud that his companions had turned to him.

After Valdy left Ollie and Lars sat quietly, watching tensely from behind the rocks with their rifles ready to shoot. They could see Valdy moving carefully into the woods, but soon he was lost from sight among the trees.

They watched nervously for almost an hour. Then with darkness beginning to fall, Valdy returned, running from tree to tree. "They've landed and they're walking along the shore, but they don't seem to have spotted the cabin. It's in shadow now and they may miss it," he reported.

"Go back up and keep watching, Lars. Valdy, stay here and guard our supplies. I'll go north to get a closer look as long as it's light enough. And remember no shooting unless we have to," Ollie announced, "and be careful not to make tracks that can be seen."

Then he carefully made his way through the woods for about a mile until he came to a clearing. A little light continued to show through the trees, and as he crouched hidden behind a large boulder he looked down at the bay where a gray powerboat lay at anchor, its machine gun pointed menacingly toward shore.

As Ollie watched his eyes became adjusted to the dimness and he could just make out several men on deck. After a short while three men appeared, walking unhurriedly along the shore carrying rifles. They reached the small boat, pushed off and slowly rowed out to the larger boat.

Ollie watched for a while and finally decided that no one else was coming ashore that night, so he made his way back to his friends.

A slight rain had begun to fall and they debated what to do. Although the temperature had warmed, the prospect of a night in the open with no fire, no tent and a freezing rain was thoroughly distasteful and starkly frightening, but they decided that a return to the cabin would be too risky. If the Germans had seen it, they might launch an attack as soon as it got light. So with the rain and darkness shrouding them, they rigged a tarpaulin between the rocks for shelter and bedded down for a cold, wet night in their blankets, feeling at least fairly safe until morning.

The next day they awoke early, cold and wet. To Ollie's amusement Valdy insisted that they must have exercises to stretch their stiff muscles. "It will make us even more stiff," Ollie argued, but Lars agreed with Valdy and they stood on the lonely hill in the remaining snow looking like dancing ghosts.

When the short exercise was over, Ollie announced, "We'll watch the

Germans again and be ready to leave if we have to. Valdy, you know the island, so why don't you go see if you can find a better hiding place on the other side of the hill. Lars, stay here and keep watching the shore near the cabin. I'll go back through the woods and keep an eye on the boat. We'll meet in three hours up at the boulders where we spent the night."

Before leaving on their missions the three men ate some bread and cheese. Feeling slightly warmer, Ollie crept through the damp woods to the previous day's vantage point where he was sheltered from the wind and from anyone on the boat who might be looking toward the shore. After what seemed like hours the small boat left the larger one again, and once more three men rowed to shore. Two of them got out of the small skiff and walked south while the third man returned to the patrol boat. He picked up two more men, and when they landed the five Germans started walking north along the shore in the opposite direction from the cabin.

Ollie returned to his companions, keeping carefully out of sight of the shore. When he got back Lars reported that the Germans had just found the cabin. They had walked around it and peered through the window and then had walked back toward the cove where their boat was beached.

Ollie immediately made his way back to his lookout point and watched the Germans returning to their vessel. The boat raised its anchor and slowly moved out of the bay toward the ocean. Apparently the enemy did not suspect anything.

Although the immediate danger was over it was agreed that they would have to post lookouts during daylight hours. But at least they could return to the cabin where they could dry out and get warm. First, however, they climbed over the hill to inspect a small cave Valdy had found. "It will be big enough for all three of us to hide in case there is another German landing," Valdy said.

Lars was beginning to become pessimistic and he growled, "Maybe more snow will make it necessary to remain longer on the island without using the cabin. At least we can build a big fire in the cave if Erik forgets to come back."

"Don't worry, Erik will come soon," Valdy said confidently.

Ollie hoped he was right. They were almost out of food, having been able to catch only a few fish, and failing to spot another deer near their hideaway. Each of them was wondering whether Erik and his crew had been captured.

Then, at last, on the nineteenth day, Erik's fishing boat slowly entered the cove. They could see him on the bridge standing tall and carefully sweeping the shoreline and woods with his binoculars. After a thorough inspection he dropped anchor and began waving his cap. The three men raced down to the shore, waving their caps to signal it was safe.

It took only a few minutes to pull their rowboat from under bushes where it had been hidden and to row out to the fishing boat. Erik, Evold and Ake greeted them warmly. Erik remarked on how thin they looked. "I think you are scarecrows to scare the Germans," he laughed.

"You get marooned next time and we will go home to food and warm beds," Valdy said angrily. "All we've eaten for four days are scraps of meat and soup made out of moss and pine needles with deer bones."

"I'm sorry, Valdy," Erik said seriously. "You know that was a bad storm. It even snowed in Bergen. And we were worried about you, but there was nothing we could do but wait and hope. The Gestapo was all over town, especially the harbor. They searched my boat twice, but not before we unloaded the cargo to Eduard's warehouse. So the Nazis found nothing on board."

Erik said, "Ake, go below and get our friends some food and coffee to warm them up."

"What about the hideout and the equipment?" Ollie asked.

"Ah, they are safe. Thor got Rolf and Kristian out of the hideout, then he worked at his father's restaurant to keep tabs on any searches by the Germans of the building. They poked around the storeroom but suspected nothing. So when you have had a couple of good meals and have caught up on sleep you can go back to work, my friend."

"We have much to tell the British," Evold said. "The Germans have started building a u-boat bunker in the harbor."

"Did the Gestapo get anyone?" Valdy asked worriedly.

It was Evold's turn to answer, and he did so with a voice so low they could hardly hear him. "Ja, they caught Carl Carlson, Knute Erickson, Lars Torberg and several others from Group 11 across the harbor according to what we have heard. That means that everyone in their group and all of their friends are in danger now."

"Fortunately none of our people were taken in, so the Germans do not know our names or where we live. But the Nazis are looking. They know someone is sending coded messages by radio to the British, and Colonel

Kraus has a top priority to catch and silence us, according to the rumor going around the harbor."

"That is bad," Valdy said. "We will be the only underground group operating in this area. That means the Gestapo can focus its attention solely on us. We will have to be even more careful, and we will have to plan a better escape network for Ollie, just in case they get close."

At that point Ake reappeared with a tray loaded with slices of bread, herring, cheese and some rare cabbage leaves, as well as steaming coffee.

"I have never been so glad to see food in my life," Ollie mumbled as he started to eat his first real meal in more than two weeks.

THOR DROVE OLLIE to Kris' modern ranch style home high up on the side of one of Bergen's hills. The view was dramatic as the sun sank on the horizon and reflected off distant roofs.

"Can we see Holsnoy from here, Thor?" Ollie asked.

"Nei, it is too far, " he answered.

After Thor rang the bell, Kris opened the door. "Now the party can start," Kris said.

Inside Kris led Ollie and Thor to the living room with light wood paneling and modern Danish furniture upholstered in brightly colored orange and green fabrics. The room had a great view from a large picture window. Ollie could see lush gardens down the hill with a profusion of colors. One corner of the room contained an electronic center with expensive looking television, radio, stereo and computer equipment, reflecting their host's business.

Erik, Rolf, and Gunnar were already seated, each wearing sports coats and ties. The men greeted one another.

"It's girls night out. I sent Olga to visit her sister in Stavanger for a few days.

Kris and Thor's wives are at a spa for the weekend," Erik said. "Just us tonight."

"And you're all dressed up with no place to go," Ollie said.

"No place yet, anyway," Erik said.

Kris handed Ollie a drink of what seemed to be a scotch sour. As he looked about him he could smell pungent fish cooking in a nearby kitchen. And hunger pangs made him realize he had had almost nothing to eat all day.

Erik, who had recovered from his hangover, began regaling the group with stories of his adventures at sea and the misadventures of other fishermen. Gunnar and Rolf yawned, having heard the tales several times before. In turn, Ollie was asked about his life and about the United States, which none of them had visited. They wanted to know if he had been to Hollywood and Disneyland, what the national parks were like, and where the best skiing could be found.

Dinner consisted of a fish soup, piles of smoked salmon, with six different dishes of herring, as well as a delicious mixed salad of peas, beans, onions and beets mixed with the lettuce and covered with sweet honey mustard dressing.

"You're a wonderful cook, Kris," Ollie told him.

"I look it, don't I," Kris said, patting his stomach.

When the meal was over, Thor brought Ollie's hanging bag inside and told him to change into dress clothes. "We're going out," Thor said.

"Fishing?" Ollie asked.

"Change and we'll talk," Thor said, leading him to a back bedroom.

Ollie put on a blazer and khaki pants. He called Polly and left a message with Erik's phone number, saying that the fishing trip was on. Then he met the other men in Kris' library where they had taken their coffee and were smoking and talking. Ollie looked out at the city from another huge picture window that faced two of the mountains across the city. They rose like sentinels under the summer night sky.

After a while, the room grew quiet. Erik stood, propped his arm on the ledge over the fireplace next to a colorful photograph of Kris with his wife and his two blond children, taken when all were much younger.

"Now, Olaf, we would like to tell you why we asked you to come back to Bergen," Erik began. "Of course we wanted to see you before we all got too old, but the real reason was because you know from personal experience about Gestapo Colonel Helmut Kraus. Well, he has returned to Bergen."

"Wait a minute, Erik," Thor interrupted from across the room where he stood tensely. "Let us go back to last year when a new German consul arrived in town. His name is Helmut Schmidt. At first none of us paid much attention to him. But Erik is an officer in the Chamber of Commerce and he met Schmidt at a reception. Now you tell Ollie what happened, Erik."

The giant nodded and the others were silent as he resumed his story in the room that now was filled with pipe tobacco smoke. "Well," he paused. "I shook hands with the consul and looked at his face. My God, I thought, he looks like that bastard Kraus back in the old days. I couldn't believe it. I thought it was a coincidence. So I mumbled a welcome. But during the evening I kept looking at him whenever I could and I was sure there was a resemblance."

Erik took a drink, relit his pipe and continued. "Then six months later Schmidt's father arrived here to live with his son. He was a retired naval historian, at least that was what they said. A few weeks later there was another large reception and I saw the old man for the first time. He is called Wolfgang Schmidt and he is in his late eighties. The more I looked the more familiar he appeared. He is Kraus. So I called The Fishermen together and told them."

Kris interrupted. "Ollie, you know Erik. He's still a hot head and we did not believe him at first, but then Thorvald was able to see Schmidt senior also. He was the only other person from our old group who had seen Kraus up close during the war, other than Ake. We did not want to get Ake involved because of the horrible memories such an encounter might bring up. Thor said that there was a definite resemblance and he thinks the old man is Kraus."

Ollie looked at Thor who said, "That is what I thought, but being a lawyer I said I wanted a better witness, someone who could testify in court. Someone who could recognize Kraus without a shadow of a doubt. That would only be you."

The story sounded plausible to Ollie, although it was disturbing. He really did not want to see the face of the very man who had stood in front of him as he screamed in pain and wet his pants after being hit with an electric cattle prod, Kraus continually demanding names, insisting on locations, vowing to kill Ollie if he didn't talk about The Fishermen's operations. Yet Ollie owed closure to the memory of Valdy, Sven, Ake and the others. He also realized that a deep, dark part of him wanted revenge. He wanted to hurt Kraus, to take away whatever dignity the Nazi might still have.

"Anyway," Kris continued, "we tried to find out what had happened to Kraus after he left here, just before the German surrender. We even hired a private investigator to search war criminal records. However, he found nothing. After the war Kraus disappeared completely. There was no record of him whatsoever. Then a Jewish group we had contacted told us they had word he fled to Argentina along with other high Nazis. But their lead turned out to be a dead end. They could not find any trace of him."

Thor took up the story. "We had some old newspaper pictures of Kraus which we blew up so that we could compare the faces. They looked alike, but we still were not one hundred percent sure. So Erik suggested that we ask you to come here again. If anyone could identify him, it would be you." He looked expectantly at Ollie.

The other men also stared at him, waiting for his reaction.

Ollie sat silently for a minute trying to digest what he had been told. Finally he said, "I don't know if I can make a positive identification after all these years. And I'm not sure that I even want to. It took many years to stop the nightmares, and now you want me to bring it all back."

His friends were silent, some of them staring at him, others looking carefully away. Finally Erik spoke. There was a hard edge to his voice. "We know what happened to you, Olaf, and we respect your feelings. But you joined us in signing an oath to find him. If it is that fucking Kraus he should be brought before a war crimes court, not just for what he did to you, but for what he did to Ake, Sven, Valdy, and hundreds of others."

"What happened to Valdy and Sven? I know they were shot in the mountains after they brought me to the Swedish border, but how did it happen?" Ollie asked in a voice that was barely audible.

The room became silent again, the men looking away from one another. No one seemed to want to speak. Finally Thorvald said, "Just after Valdy and Sven left you, Sven saw a German ski patrol in the distance, so the two split up to try to distract the Germans from detecting you. The Germans spotted them and Sven tried to race down a long glacial slope. But one of their marksmen shot him in the leg. Still he kept going and almost got away but he lost a lot of blood in the process. At one point he came too close to a steep slope and he fell at the edge trying to stop, but by then he was weak. He pitched down the mountain and started a small avalanche that carried him to the bottom of the slope and broke his skis. He was covered by snow but able to move his arms enough to punch an air hole through the snow with a ski pole. No one heard his cries for help, though, until the next day when a forest ranger saw his broken skis and dug him out."

Thor said that the ranger skied to the nearest town only a few miles away and organized some local patriots to come with him to rescue Sven. They strapped him to a sled and brought him to their village, where they hid him. But the town was small and isolated and without a doctor. Sven was not strong enough to travel so the villagers tried to nurse him. But gradually he lost his strength and ten days later he died. Before he became too weak to speak, he told a woman about his escape and she told the ranger, who came to Bergen after the war and told The Fishermen the story.

The old Fishermen sat still, no one talking. Ollie shook his head in sorrow. Long ago Erik had written him that the Germans had killed Sven and Valdy but he had not included the details and Ollie had not been bold or brave enough to ask. Now, finally, after all the years, Ollie learned how loyal Sven had been to him, diverting the Nazis in order to save him. In a tense voice Ollie asked, "What about Valdy? What happened to him?"

Erik cleared his throat. Then he said, "We heard the story at the end of the war from a German prisoner who had been a member of the ski patrol that saw Valdy and Sven. He told us that Valdy had slalomed down the mountain in full view toward the patrol, almost as if he was showing off. What a great ballet skier he was, the prisoner said. When Valdy was perhaps two hundred yards away from the patrol, he turned suddenly, racing straight downhill at a great speed. The German said that they had never seen such skiing. It was as if Valdy was challenging them to a race. The patrol tried to follow him and they fired their guns at him without success because they kept falling further and further behind. The German prisoner said that he almost wished that Valdy had gotten away because he was so beautiful against the snow. But the rest of the patrol was further down the mountain and, unknowingly, Valdy skied right to them."

Erik wiped his nose with the palm of his hand, then continued, "One of the Germans shot him in the hip. That's how they finally captured him. They had orders from Kraus to take prisoners and to use all methods of interrogation to make them talk. But even though Valdy must have been in terrible pain, he did not say anything. They hung him from a tree by a rope cinched under his arms and beat him with branches. After that they removed his boots and beat the soles of his feet, but still he was silent. The German said that Valdy hung there all afternoon in the wind and freezing temperatures and that they kept beating him until he lost consciousness. Finally they just left him and went back to their camp."

Erik's voice choked and he stopped to regain his composure. "Now you know why we want to capture Kraus. He told his men to do anything to the prisoners to make them talk. They showed no mercy to anyone."

"Valdy was like a brother to me while I was in Norway. He saved my life. Sven did too," Ollie finally said in a whisper. "I'll try to identify this man you feel is Kraus. But how am I to get close to him? I can't very well wait outside the consul's house until he leaves on an errand or goes on a walk."

"Simple," Kris replied. "There's a big reception tonight. Bergen is getting a new television channel and the Chamber of Commerce is sponsoring a reception to celebrate the event. All the local bigwigs will be there, including the Schmidts, because the Germans own the new station." He grinned his old mischievous smile. "And I have obtained an invitation for you, Ollie. It's why we needed you to get here so quickly. There will be a receiving line that you and I will go through, shaking hands with all the dignitaries. You'll come face to face with the man we think is Kraus."

"And if I can identify him, what then?" Ollie demanded.

It was Erik's turn to grin. "You will signal Thor. Then he will come outside the hall and give a signal to us. Rolf, Gunnar and I will be waiting across the street. We will drive to the consul's house where we will wait in the dark. When they get out of their car we will surprise them, as if mugging them, only instead of taking a wallet we'll capture Kraus. We'll drive him to a safe house we've set up where we can hide and interrogate him until we are one hundred percent sure we have the right person. Then we will fly him to Oslo in Kris' private plane and we'll turn him over to the proper authorities for an official war crimes trial. Easy, Olaf, you'll see," he said confidently.

"Easy?" Ollie asked. "You could create an international incident. Not to mention the fact that you'll be breaking any number of laws along the way."

"That's a risk we must take for justice," Thor replied. "Before we turn Kraus in I will contact a friend in our justice department and obtain a promise that Kraus will be tried. And if we do not obtain a firm commitment, we will go to the British. If they say no, we go to your embassy. And if they do not want to try Kraus, we talk with the Russians. Our last resort will be the Israelis. They would love to find Kraus and bring him to trial for what he did to Norwegian Jews during the war. But working with the Israelis would present logistical problems and it would be expensive. Mossad is experienced, though, and tough. They would cooperate because Kraus is one of the last major Nazi war criminals still at large. They will want to try him if he can be brought to Israel."

"I could be disbarred over all this," Ollie said.

"We're not asking you to break any laws," Erik said.

"We just need you to identify him at the reception," Thor replied.

"If I am certain it's him, you must promise me that there will be no torture or revenge," Ollie said.

"I say we make him talk, no matter what, even if we have to use his own methods, which we remember all too well," Erik challenged.

Thor glared at Erik.

"He would be a very old man now and it would be easy to bring on a heart attack or stroke," Ollie said. "If this plan goes awry, you could be charged with not only kidnapping but murder."

"How can that bastard have a heart attack? He doesn't have a heart," Erik said. "That piece of shit deserves no sympathy. He never showed it to anyone else."

"I can't join in a plan that involves Nazi-like brutality," Ollie said. "As much as I would love to see him hung by his balls, that would make us just as immoral as the Germans were."

Thorvald, always the most thoughtful and gentle member of The Fishermen, said, "I think most of us agree with you. We want justice to be meted out if it is warranted and that means that if the man really is Kraus, he must be captured and brought to a fair trial, without violence."

"Then I'll try to get a good look at him," Ollie said. "But that's all."

"Okay?" Thor asked, looking around at the other men who all nodded in agreement. Everyone, Ollie noticed, except Erik.

...

The large, brightly-lit ballroom was decorated with balloons and Norwegian and German flags. "I still get mad when I see a German flag," Kris whispered to Ollie as he, Ollie, and Thor entered the crowded ballroom.

While they stood for a minute inside the doorway Ollie asked, "Will I know anyone besides you two?"

"Eduard, who stored the fish we caught and hid your equipment, and Knute, you remember him? He was the little man who was studying to be an engineer. Now he is on the Bergen city council. Remember, he was always telling jokes," Thor said. "Kris will take you to the receiving line. If you identify Kraus, you will button your suit jacket, then nod to me. I will be nearby. That will be the confirmation. I'll go to outside and light a cigarette. That will be the signal for Erik and the others. If he is not Kraus, you will simply turn away and get a drink. I'll go to the door, shake my head, and won't light a cigarette. That will be the end and you will have had a nice vacation in Bergen visiting old friends."

"But I am sure he is Kraus, I feel it in my bones," Kris said softly. " My arthritis tells me so."

"Let's find out," Ollie replied as the three walked into the ballroom at the Hotel Norge, which was crowded with dignitaries and conservatively dressed business leaders accompanied by their more brightly clothed spouses. It could have been a convention or party at the Fairmont in San Francisco, Ollie thought. They were all was chatting and gesturing at once, trying to keep from spilling their drinks.

With the noise roaring in his ears, Ollie felt claustrophobic as people pushed past him to greet friends and to impress others with their importance. There was no one he recognized at the reception aside from The Fishermen he had been with during the previous day, all of whom had spoken English to him. But Norwegian was being spoken rapidly all around him and he could not understand any of it. It had been so long since he had heard the language.

"I'll catch up with you later," Thor said to Kris and Ollie. "Good luck."

Ollie watched Thor walk to a group of people that included Eduard.

"Let's start with a drink," Kris said. And with a sly smile he asked, "Do you still like aquavit?"

Ollie remembered the strong sensation of the burning liqueur at Erik's party. "I'll pass on that," he said, moving into the ballroom with Kris. He had a strange feeling of detachment from the whole situation, which was welcome considering the assignment he had accepted.

Kris and Ollie elbowed their way toward one of the crowded bars where, after waiting in line, they were finally able to obtain drinks. Ollie asked the bartender in English for a weak Scotch and soda and received some kind of rum concoction with a slice of pineapple. Kris ended up with an unidentifiable tall drink decorated with a paper umbrella.

On their way to the receiving line Kris began introducing Ollie as his cousin, visiting from America, to people in the crowd. Ollie vaguely caught the names of a man who was in the import/export business, the owner of an art gallery, a woman who raised horses. And then, Ollie realized, he and Kris were at the start of the receiving line.

Ollie shook hands with the television station manager, two members of the ownership group, and the mayor, who was holding court with several other people.

"Ah, an American," he said to Ollie with a slight smile, and then he turned toward the next person without waiting for a reply.

Ollie was amused. He did not vote in Bergen, so apparently he was not important enough for the mayor to waste time on while there were other local hands to shake. Out of the corner of his eye Ollie could see that Thor was shadowing him, watching as unobtrusively as possible.

Kris introduced Ollie to two of the news anchors. Afterward Kris turned to Ollie and said, "Here comes our man."

Ollie looked beyond a small cluster of people surrounding a tall, handsome man with a ramrod posture, closely cropped graying hair, and a diplomatic red sash across his formal dinner jacket. Next to him was an equally tall, frail, older man with thinning gray, cropped hair, a tight-lipped smile and stooped shoulders. He stared vacantly at everyone who was being introduced.

Feeling nervous and almost relieved Ollie followed his old comrade to meet the consul.

"Ah, my friend, Kris," the German official said in English when he saw them. "I am happy you could come tonight. What a wonderful occasion this is. I am so happy that a German corporation could be one of the prime contractors for Bergen's new television station. Bergen is one of my favorite cities in all the world."

Ollie had the urge to ask whether that included cities in Argentina and Chile, where Kraus reportedly had lived with his family after 1945.

"Good evening, Helmut, I am honored that I could join the celebration. It is a wonderful occasion, and the new television station should bring in much business. I will use it for advertising," Kris replied warmly. "But now I want you to meet my cousin who is visiting us. This is Olaf Larsen, a very distinguished American attorney. He was head of the California bar two years ago."

Ollie smiled and wondered why Kris had fabricated the extra California bar status for him. He had never been anything in the bar except a member of an inactive committee on legal ethics.

"It is an honor to meet you, Consul," Ollie said. "My cousin has told me how much you are doing to build commerce between Bergen and Germany."

As he spoke he studied the man's face, and, yes, he knew why his friends said that he looked like Kraus had so many years ago. There were the same high cheekbones, straight nose, and tight lips.

"It is a pleasure to meet you, Mr. Larsen, but I have done nothing very special, just the usual work of a consul. And, of course, it is so easy in this friendly, beautiful city. But I want you both to meet my father, Wolfgang Schmidt, who is living with us. He is a naval historian and a retired professor. Father, this is my good friend Kris Svenson and his American cousin, Mr. Larsen."

The older man held out his hand automatically and shook Ollie's hand with a strong grip. He looked at Ollie politely with no sign of recognition or special interest.

In return Ollie stared at the consul's father, searching for features that could be recalled despite the wrinkles that had come with age. The old man's eyes still were clear blue with a slight squint behind steel-framed glasses. Kraus had not worn glasses during the German occupation of Bergen. The man's eyes moved nervously from side to side and were slightly watery. They looked the same shape and color as Kraus's had.

The nose was long and wide, though a bit fleshy. Ollie and Colonel Kraus had stared at each other for hours on end for three days while the Gestapo officer's aides applied different tortures. Now the face was slightly familiar, but Ollie was not a hundred percent certain.

Then he saw a small mole beside the nose. A coincidence? He studied the pronounced high cheekbones and thin lips. And finally he noted a tiny scar on the left side of the chin. It was barely visible, but Ollie remembered it well. He had stared at it while Kraus was interrogating him for those three miserable days so long ago, demanding the names of The Fishermen and where they broadcast. Studying the scar had helped him keep his concentration during the intense questioning, and now he wondered why Kraus had not had a better job of plastic surgery. Maybe it was at the end of the war and he could not find a Nazi doctor. It would have been simple, but it was obvious from the drawn skin that he also had had a facelift, even though it had not been expertly performed.

Ollie felt himself staring. He wondered if Kraus would recognize him as well.

"As a naval historian you must enjoy living here with the lovely harbor and so many ships from every maritime nation, and the wonderful Viking heritage," he said slowly in English while trying to sound casual though his heart was pounding. He wanted to scream, "Nazi pig, fucking Nazi bastard." But Ollie held his fury in. He knew it was not the time or place to confront Kraus.

"Ja, ja, Bergen is sehr hübsch. I like Norway and I like the sea," the old man replied with slight animation. He showed no sign of recognizing Ollie.

At that point several other people approached to be introduced and Kris and Ollie retreated. Ollie wanted to shout and reveal the truth about his former enemy, and he wanted to punch the old man and kick him in the head. Instead he felt his stomach burn with acid and he thought for a moment that he might throw up.

"Well?" Kris asked.

Ollie turned toward Thor, who was standing a few feet away, and then Ollie buttoned his suit jacket and nodded his head. Thor's eyes widened. He nodded back. Then Ollie whispered to Kris, "Finally, that fucking bastard will be handed over to the war crimes trial people," as he watched Thor hurry to the door.

Ollie wondered whether Kraus was an excellent poker player who could hide his thoughts, or whether the old man really did not know him. Maybe the colonel's mind had slipped. Or were there so many torture victims that one would not stand out enough for recognition after more than fifty years?

But there was no question who the man was. Ollie knew beyond any doubt that this was Kraus, the Gestapo officer of World War II, the torturer, who had almost killed him, who had sent Bergen's Jews to concentration camps, who was responsible for Ake's crippling and Valdy's terrible death. Ollie wanted to smash his fist into the hated face.

The rest of the evening was a dull blur for Ollie as he and Kris mingled. Ollie tried to make small talk with other guests but few spoke English and he was preoccupied. He wondered whether Kraus might realize that they had met before. He also worried about the kidnapping plans. Could his old friends accomplish it without a fight? Could they make Kraus talk without using force? Were they too old to act as a commando team hiding in wait to spring an ambush? They were all fools and would all be arrested, he was sure. He thought of calling off the whole project, but he realized it was too late. His friends already had left for the consul's house. By the time Kris and Ollie watched the consul and his father leave the ballroom, the atmosphere had become stifling—crowded, overheated, and smoke-filled. Ollie welcomed Kris' instruction that they leave as well.

"My God, I've never heard Norwegians talk so much and say so little," Kris said as they made their way through the crowd. "Usually we are a quiet people, but a large group celebrating with free drinks makes us loud and uninhibited."

Outside it was still light from the midnight sun, even though it was nearly eleven o'clock. On the sidewalk, they met up with Thor, who whispered, "Are you positive, Ollie?"

"Yes, there is no doubt. I only wonder why the plastic surgeons did not do a better job on him. There still are definite features that have not changed. They give him away. The nose is fleshy now, but the basic shape is the same. There's still a small mole and a tiny scar on the chin."

Thor was quiet as they walked toward his car. "Not the usual German efficiency," he said, inserting his key in the lock and opening the door. "I wondered the same thing when I saw him several weeks ago. I was sure it was Kraus and that he'd had a face job. Maybe over the years in Argentina he grew to feel sure that no one would recognize him since the international community in Argentina hadn't known him before the war. He may have assumed he didn't need the pain and inconvenience of further surgery."

Once inside Thor's Volvo, Kris used his cell phone to call Erik's mobile.

"They're on their way now," Kris told him.

"We can't thank you enough for helping us," Thor said as he pulled the car onto the street.

"My pleasure, believe me," Ollie told him.

"So now you have a few days to relax at Erik's house before going home," Thor said. "And you will have had a nice vacation in Bergen visiting friends."

"Do I remember you mentioning that you wanted to look up a friend in Kirkenes?" Kris asked.

Ollie felt a flutter of adrenaline, followed by a wave of guilt. "It was an offhanded remark," he said. "I don't expect you to go to the trouble."

"You haven't come all this way to sit in Erik's house," Kris said. "You'll have a free day tomorrow and I'll have my pilot take you."

Ollie nodded his head. He couldn't argue with the generous offer.

The men were silent as Thor drove the winding road up to Erik's house. Ollie looked out the window at the harbor that glinted in the light. The light, Ollie thought. Everything was visible in the summer Norwegian light, nothing could hide for long. He remembered Erik at Kris' house, how he seemed to be trying to hide his intentions but how visible they had seemed to Ollie. "Tell me again the plan from here for Kraus," Ollie asked.

"We will try to make him answer questions, leading him on slowly," Thor said.

"But if that does not work, there's always subtle persuasion," Kris added.

"That's what I'm worried about," Ollie said.

"But we all agreed there will be no violence," Thor told him.

"Everyone except Erik," Ollie said. "I was watching him. I don't trust him. I want to go to the safe house with you."

"Are you sure?" Thor asked.

"I have to go, just to be sure," he told them before Thor made a U-turn in the road and headed in the opposite direction.

chapter six

SEPTEMBER 1942-JANUARY 1943

SIX MONTHS AFTER he evaded the Germans on Holsnoy, Ollie, Knute, Karl, and Rolf climbed one of the seven hills surrounding Bergen to repair a damaged transmitter hidden on the summit in an outcropping of rocks. Knute and Rolf stood watch at the edge of the nearby woods as Ollie and Karl worked. A few birds sang to each other in the distance. The late afternoon sun warmed Ollie's shirt, making him a little drowsy and more relaxed than he'd been in a year.

He didn't hear the German patrol until a soldier shouted, "*Bewegen Sie nicht*," from behind him. Knute and Rolf ran into the woods and escaped while Karl told Ollie to stand still.

A dozen German soldiers dressed in mountain camouflage uniforms circled the two Fishermen. They all had rifles that they pointed at Karl and Ollie, but they seemed nervous, looking around as if searching for other people on the mountain. The officer in charge had a large pistol hanging from his belt. He was a red-faced man with a deep, gravelly voice and he said something to Karl and Ollie in German.

"He told us to put our hands on our heads or they'll shoot," Karl said to Ollie. The two men quickly complied with the order.

Ollie and Karl were marched down the mountain, then blindfolded and taken away, each in separate cars. Ollie never saw Karl again.

The Gestapo held Ollie for almost a week while Kraus and his fat lieutenant, Ulrich Schnips, questioned him about the broadcasts and his work as a spy. After the first day, when Ollie refused to say more than his name, rank, and serial number, they began torturing him. Red-hot pokers were held against his bare feet causing large blisters to form. Schnips thought it was funny. He laughed loudly when Ollie screamed. Ollie watched the man's fat belly bouncing with laughter until he had to close his eyes against the pain. Later, Schnips bent his thumbs back until they touched his wrists. Kraus repeatedly shocked him with an electric cattle prod.

At a point, while Ollie was hunched over in a chair and Kraus was holding the point of a knife next to Ollie's eye and threatening to blind him, Ollie heard two loud explosions.

"Was ist dies?" Kraus asked Schnips, who shook his head. The two men rushed from the room.

Moments later Ollie heard shouting and suddenly a group of men in black clothing with ski masks over their faces stormed into the room.

"He's here," one shouted, lifting him from a chair and carrying him outside, where Ollie was placed on a stretcher. The stretcher-bearers ran down Kong Oscarsgate.

"We are sorry to jostle you, Olaf, but we must get away as fast as we can," Ollie heard Evold say. With each bump the pain almost made Ollie faint, but he clenched his teeth and took deep breaths trying to remain conscious, scared and bewildered, but still conscious.

Ollie's rescuers took him to Ake's nearby small apartment on the north edge of town. The house was owned by Gunnar's father and was used occasionally by The Fishermen when they wanted to meet far from the center of town, or in emergencies.

Ake had a bedroom and a small living room. The walls were gray with flaking paint, and the furniture was old and scuffed. Above the bed there was a crucifix. One wall had travel posters for trips to the northern fjords and on another wall there was a picture of the holy family with Mary holding the baby Jesus. In the corner was a table. Across the room there was a small refrigerator, hot plate, and a sink.

The second room had an old couch that was made up into a bed, covered with a torn slipcover. The room also had a table and three straight-backed wooden chairs as well as a floor lamp that provided barely enough light to read by.

Evold and Erik helped Ollie lie down on the couch. Then Erik turned to Ake. "You remember," he said, pointing at the shorter man. "You will say nothing about this to anyone. Do you understand? Nothing! You must be quiet or you might endanger all our lives. You go into no bars and you stay sober. If you get drunk and start talking and tell anyone, I mean anyone, that Ollie is with you, I will personally break every bone in your fucking body, old friend," Erik had warned.

"I know what you mean, Erik, old friend," Ake had replied seriously, and for the next month he did not touch a drop of liquor. His only responsibility was to care for Ollie, applying ointments to the cattle prod burns, changing the bandages around the stick splints that Thor had fashioned on Ollie's broken thumbs, and feeding him, although Erik took Ake out fishing several times just so that his routine would appear normal. However, after five days, Ollie rebelled and told Thor, who had come to check on his health, that the diet of fried fish, greasy potatoes and onions was making him sick. He said the smell was as hard to endure as the German torture had been. After that Thor, Eduard and Sven began a daily shuttle of edible food from Thorvald's father's restaurant.

A month later, Erik, Thor, Valdy, and Sven appeared one evening at dark and Erik announced that they would move Ollie the next day to a small village further north, off a tributary of the Sognefjord. There Ollie would be safer and could go out walking to build up his legs so eventually he would be able to climb the mountains and escape across the border into Sweden. Ollie had been fighting boredom and had run out of conversation with his well-intentioned host. He welcomed the news of moving and looked forward to a new place to hide. And then Valdy set a Bible on a table near Ollie and Erik produced a pen knife that the five men used to prick their fingers, sealing in their own blood on the Bible an oath to bring Kraus to justice.

...

On a cold and snowy November day, Erik and Evold helped Ollie walk up a path from a small dock to a neat white farmhouse with blue trim around the windows. They were met at the door by the farmer, Olaus Pederson, his wife Marta, and their daughter, Kirsten.

Ollie stared at the young woman, thinking she was the most beautiful girl he had ever seen. Her auburn hair cascaded to her shoulders. Her cheeks were white with a touch of pink. He realized he was gawking and made himself turn toward the mother, a pleasant looking and slightly plump lady. She smiled at him.

The farmer stepped forward to shake Ollie's hand with an iron grip that made him wince. Olaus was a large man wearing a leather jacket and high boots. "I saw your boat coming but I was too slow to meet you at the dock, so I say velkommen here instead."

From where they all stood Ollie could see the farm consisted of a wooded hillside, pasture, three Jersey cows in a corral attached to a red barn, and the farmhouse with a hen house right next to it.

"We have prepared a room for you in the barn," Olaus said cheerfully. "Erik, you will help me move the bed and ladder. We have put a lamp, chairs and table there so you will be a little comfortable while you get well."

"We would give you our son's room," Olaus's wife said with some embarrassment, "but it might be dangerous because sometimes we have visitors and a stranger would bring suspicion."

Ollie suddenly realized what a risk these people would be taking in harboring him.

"Kirsten will teach you how to milk cows and make butter," Olaus said, "and when you are stronger you can help me get the heavy milk cans onto the wagon and the boat. We will teach you about farming." He gave Ollie a big smile.

"I already know a little," Ollie said, blushing slightly. "We fatten steers for market at my parents' farm in Minnesota."

"Ha, that is funny. You teach me." Olaus laughed loudly.

Two weeks later, Ollie held Kirsten for the first time in his arms.

"My father will not like this," she said with a smile. "Since my brother is away with the army, my father almost thinks of you as a son. We should not kiss but I am so lonely. All the young men from here and my friends stay in the town. They are afraid to go out because of the Germans."

Ollie sensed her need for love and companionship, and he knew that he had been repressing the loneliness he felt being so far away from his family and friends. "Can I be your friend?" he asked softly. When she smiled he blurted out, "You are so beautiful and I think I love you." He was instantly both embarrassed and happy.

She lifted her hand to his face and laid it against his cheek. "I love you also, Olaf. You are very brave, and you are very gentle."

"Will you come to the loft with me?" he asked, barely daring to breathe. She smiled and when she pulled him toward the ladder he felt a rush of excitement.

Ollie stayed in a room off the hayloft, a place where grain was once stored. After they climbed the ladder he shut the door to the room for an extra measure of privacy. Kirsten took his blankets from his narrow cot and spread them on the floor. They lay down together, kissing and touching each other slowly at first and then urgently. He pulled Kirsten's sweater over her head and slowly unbuttoned her shirt, finding she was not wearing a brassiere. He kissed her soft breasts.

Kirsten undid the buttons on his pants and laughing, they took off each other's shoes. And then he couldn't wait any longer. He rolled on top of her and pushed into her moist, warm vagina. Kirsten gave a little cry and pulled him tightly to her.

As they rested a little later, Ollie said, "I hope I didn't hurt you."

She shook her head and smiled, and kissed him again passionately.

"I hope I was not too quick, but I could not stop."

"I loved it. I've never had such exciting loving," Kirsten whispered between kisses and began running her hand over his body.

This time it was slower and gentler, and Ollie could feel Kirsten quiver as she had one orgasm after another. And later there was a third time. But when it was over, Kirsten told him she had to go before her parents wondered where she was. She dressed quickly and paused at the ladder for a final kiss. She promised to come back to him the next night.

For the next two months Kirsten came to the barn every evening with his dinner and they talked. She told him about her hope of going to the university some day. She said she wanted to be an art teacher, and she did not want to live all her life in the country. Instead she wanted to move to Oslo or maybe to Bergen or Trondheim where there would be more people and cultural events.

Ollie replied that he, too, did not want to live in the country, and he described Minneapolis, where he had gone to college, and Duluth, where he had worked one summer.

They were in the barn's loft the night Kirsten told him they had learned that the Germans had captured her brother. She proudly showed him a picture of a handsome young soldier. All her family knew was that he was in a prisoner of war camp.

"Almost everyone in Norway hates the Germans," she spat angrily. "We all have relatives or friends who have been captured. And we hear about things that the Gestapo do, like what they did to you. We want to help no matter how dangerous it is."

After that, in the days ahead when they talked, they kept their arms around each other. She would be so serious, then very suddenly think of something funny and burst out in loud laughter. He loved her perfect white teeth.

As Ollie got better, Kirsten took him out skiing. He used her brother's skis and boots. She showed him the trail he would take to escape over the mountains to Sweden. And she helped him improve his cross-country skiing. Every day they skied and his strength returned. In the evening they talked about the future.

And then on a clear night with a full moon, Evold, Valdy, and Sven appeared in the barn without warning, waking Ollie from his sleep. Valdy and Sven were dressed all in white and held a rucksack of white ski clothes for Ollie as well as a sleeping bag, ground cloth, and food. They also handed him photographs and maps showing a hidden German laboratory and production plant used to produce heavy water that would help the Nazis in making a super bomb. The men told Ollie that it was critical information that could not be sent by radio but must be delivered by hand at all costs so that the Nazis could be stopped. Halting heavy water production had become the Allies' main objective in Norway, his friends told him.

As Ollie was changing into the white ski pants and jacket, Evold left to return to his boat and sail back to Bergen, but Valdy and Sven stayed with Ollie and helped him pack up his gear. After midnight, with the moon shining brightly, Ollie was ready to leave and knocked on the door of the farmhouse to say a sudden farewell to the Pedersons. The farmer shook his hand, the wife hugged him, and then Kirsten told her parents she would walk Ollie to the trail. She was wearing a coat over her flannel nightgown and began shivering, or at least Ollie thought she was shivering. As he put his arm around her shoulder, he realized she was sobbing. He kissed her head as they walked. He told her that he would return.

"We'll get married when this is all over," he said. "I'll always love you."

She clung to him all the way to the trail, where Valdy and Sven were waiting in their white ski clothes, like the ptarmigan whose feathers went white in winter to blend in with the snow and camouflage it from predators. The men needed any advantage to keep the German patrols from seeing them. Ollie and Kirsten kissed one last time before she turned and ran back to the farmhouse. Ollie watched her dark figure against the white snow, her hair blowing up and down delicately, like silk cloth.

When she was out of sight, Valdy said, "She's a beautiful girl. When you go home, you will have at least one happy memory of Norway."

As he strapped on his skis and slipped the pack's straps over his shoulders, Ollie kept his head down so his friends wouldn't see the tears that filled his eyes.

"We have a long trek ahead," Valdy said.

"And difficult," Sven told him as the three men looked up the slope.

"I hope I can make it up the mountain with this heavy rucksack. It looks steeper tonight," Ollie said, trying to keep his voice under control.

"We will help you, Olaf," Sven said. "You know that Valdy is our champion cross-country skier and will win the next Olympics, if there is a next Olympics."

Valdy looked away and answered, "I am not so good. Sven is good. He is a great slalom racer and a fine jumper. He has skied and hiked these mountains since he was a boy and he knows the easiest way past the glaciers."

"It feels like it's getting colder," Ollie told them.

"It probably will go well below freezing up high tonight, I think," Sven said. "It is good that it is cold, for not many Germans will be in the mountains watching the border. They probably will stay in their warm quarters through the night, and we should have a few hours without needing to worry."

Ollie glanced back quickly once more, then they began their climb—alternating between sidestepping up the steepest sections, running with their skis in a V position on medium grade slopes, and gliding and sliding through more level parts. With every step Ollie wanted to turn around and ski in the opposite direction, straight to the Pederson's farm. He had to fight to keep from racing back to Kirsten, but he had to get the information to the British and he didn't want to put the Pedersons in any more danger.

It was a difficult climb and soon Ollie was fighting for breath. The freezing air at the higher altitude seared his lungs. He worried that his muscles would tighten up because he still wasn't in top shape. Even though he had skied with Kirsten for weeks, Ollie was afraid he wasn't strong enough yet to make the whole journey. And as the men climbed, Ollie kept thinking of Kirsten, which took his mind off the mountain, the physical pain he felt, and the dangers ahead.

At one difficult point Valdy and Sven got far ahead and Ollie could not see them when the wind created a curtain of snowflakes that impaired his vision. He felt alone and frightened. What would happen if he were permanently separated from his experienced companions? He had been trained for boats and landings, not for mountains or blizzards. Could he survive if the weather turned worse? Would he become disoriented with no recognizable landmarks to guide him?

He focused on completing his mission—the powerful responsibility of trying to sidetrack the mysterious heavy water project. He tried unsuccessfully to remember college physics, which had been one of his worst classes. What he did understand was that if the Germans could develop a super bomb, they would use it to destroy Britain and end the war.

That was all Ollie knew, but it was enough to motivate him. He had to succeed. He carried maps and photographs that could be used in efforts to sabotage the plant. Ollie had to get across the border to neutral Sweden and then to England or his whole stay in Norway would have little meaning for the Allies. So he hiked on despite the fear and pain. Soon he met his two companions, who had stopped a few hundred yards ahead to wait for him. They ate a quick snack of dried fruit, cheese, bread, and smoked fish to give them the energy to press on.

When they resumed their journey the sun was just beginning to creep over the mountains from the east, making the snow shimmer blue and purple as it lit the frigid landscape.

chapter seven

THOR DROVE THROUGH the woods up a hill outside of Bergen. He'd tuned in a classical radio station and the men were listening to a lively folk piece by Grieg when the music was interrupted. The announcer spoke slowly and seriously.

"Ah, the word is out," Thor said.

"What? What is it?" Ollie asked.

"Breaking news," Thor said, turning up the volume.

"The authorities have been notified of Schmidt's kidnapping," Kris said, translating for Ollie as Thor turned off on a narrow, bumpy dirt road. The night had finally grown dark.

"How much do the police know?" Ollie asked.

"No clear descriptions of the kidnappers but they're asking people to look for Schmidt, an elderly man with short gray hair and glasses," Kris said.

Thor laughed. "That could describe me," he said, as the music began again.

After another fifteen minutes of driving over rocks, through slippery ruts and down a muddy path that had not been graded since the last rain, they arrived at a small log cabin. It was hidden in a grove of pine trees. One room was lit and Erik's car was parked out of direct sight in a two-car garage attached to the rear of the cabin.

As they stepped out of the car Ollie could feel the cool night air, and he shivered. Whether it was from the temperature or excitement, he did not know, but suddenly he remembered feeling cold during most of his sojourn in Norway. For an instant he held his arms across his chest to help keep warm. And for no reason, he thought of Kirsten and how they had held each other at night to keep warm and because they wanted to touch each other. Then he thought of Polly, and briefly felt guilty that he had been thinking again of his old love instead of his devoted wife.

When they reached the cabin, Rolf was sitting outside the door next to a small box.

"You decided to join us," Rolf said to Ollie.

"I changed my mind," Ollie told him.

"Did everything go well?" Kris asked.

"Perfectly, all according to plan," Rolf said. "We hid in the bushes and took the consul and Kraus completely by surprise when they got out of their car. We had our guns out and the consul was too scared to try anything. He knew it was no joke and all he could do was stand there saying, 'No, no.'"

"We heard a news report on the radio," Thor said.

"We figured word would spread fast," Rolf told him, reaching down and taking ski masks from the box and handing the masks to Thor, Kris, and Ollie. "They're ready for you, whenever you are."

The three men pulled the ski masks over their heads then Thor knocked loudly on the door using The Fishermen's old secret signal. Gunnar opened the door, leading into a large log cabin. At least Ollie thought the man was Gunnar because he, too, wore a ski mask over his head. In fact, the three other men in the room all wore ski masks. Only Kraus' face was visible. He sat almost motionless in a torn upholstered chair in the middle of the room, staring toward the door as if trying to recognize the new arrivals. He appeared pale and frightened as he faced his masked captors.

As Ollie's eyes became accustomed to the dim light, he looked quickly around the room, bare except for a rug, a table with a tape recorder in front of Kraus, and several old wooden chairs. Reindeer antlers were mounted on three walls, a large rifle was propped against one wall, and Ollie concluded that this was a hunting lodge. A bright spotlight had been rigged up in advance and the biggest Fisherman—Nils, Ollie believed—turned it on so that it shone in Kraus' face. The German squinted and wiped his face with a handkerchief.

"The prosecutor is here," another Fisherman said. It was Erik, Ollie realized. "We'll begin now," he said.

Thor sat in a chair across the table, facing the prisoner. He motioned for Ollie to sit in the chair to his right. Kris sat in the chair to his left and turned on the tape recorder. The three other men stood behind Kraus.

Ollie looked around at his old companions. With the ski masks on he could recognize the pronounced features of his companions: Erik's strong jaw, Lars' high cheekbones, Nils' large head, and Kris' toothy smile. Thor wore his eyeglasses beneath the mask, the frames pulling the material out, like some bulging-eyed bug.

"This meeting is being recorded on July 27, in the year 1998," Thor said in English. "For security reasons, my companions and I will address each other by a letter of the alphabet. I am T., and I will start the questions for our prisoner," Thor said to the machine.

Thor studied Kraus for several minutes without saying anything more. Then he began. "You are really Helmut Kraus, not Wolfgang Schmidt, yes?"

Kraus put his hands over his face to block out the spotlight but said nothing.

"You were a Gestapo colonel in charge of central Norway during World War II. Is that correct?" Thor asked.

Kraus looked down at the table, his pale blue eyes blinking, but he remained silent.

"You see, Herr Kraus, we know much about you. We know what you did from 1940 to 1944," Thor explained. "Like you, we are historians, and we want to set the wartime record straight for future generations."

Kraus sat stiffly in his chair, seeming to ignore the questions. The only sign that he might be nervous was his breathing, which was deep and rapid. Instead of watching his captors, he sat staring at the tape recorder.

"You came to Bergen in 1940 after the German invasion of Norway," Thor said. "Your primary assignments were to control the underground forces, to prevent sabotage and halt communication with the British, and to send local Jews to concentration camps. Your headquarters were on Kong Oscarsgate, Number 27. Is that correct?"

Kraus tried to look through the light at the man who was questioning him. For the first time his face showed some concern, although he remained silent with lips compressed.

"We remember what you did to some of our friends," Thor continued in a soft voice. "We know about the tortures. We do not want to use the same methods, but we will if we must. Remember what you did to Norwegian prisoners, Herr Kraus? Do you feel any remorse or guilt? You violated the Geneva Convention agreement on the care of war prisoners."

The room was silent, with Ollie and the Norwegians waiting patiently and somberly. Tension filled the air. Ollie noticed that several of his friends were clenching their fists as if they were holding themselves back from pouncing on the prisoner.

"Would you like some coffee or wine to calm yourself, Herr Kraus?" Kris asked in a friendly manner, acting as the good guy. Ollie could see that he was smiling under his mask.

The prisoner shook his head and blinked again through watery eyes. "Who are you? What do you want?" he finally asked in a faltering voice.

"We are veterans of the war. We have long memories. We seek the truth," Thor said. "Tell us, Herr Kraus. Tell us what your orders were. Who did you report to? How did you make people talk?" Thor's voice suddenly became hard and he stressed the word 'you.'

"Like you, we are historians," he said a second time. Kraus did not react.

"I am innocent," Kraus finally answered in a whisper. "You must have the wrong man. My name is Wolfgang Schmidt. I am the consul's father. I am not a member of the Gestapo."

"You tortured your prisoners. You were a sadist, and you violated the Geneva Convention," Thor said, leaning against the table and pointing his finger toward Kraus.

"I knew nothing of the Geneva Convention in those days," Kraus answered. "And we did nothing that the Americans and British did not do."

"Liar," Ollie said, the word spitting from his mouth as he rose from his chair.

Thor put his hand on Ollie's shoulder and shook his head at him. Ollie sat down again as Thor turned back to Kraus. "Do you really believe that we don't know? What the Nazis did was a hundred times worse than anything the Allies did." He stood up and pressed his hands against the table while staring down at the old man for several minutes. "Do you really believe that?" he said again, then shook his head.

"No," Kraus said. "I know nothing. I was not there."

After another pause Thor turned away and nodded to Erik. "My large friend, E. here, is not so nice as I am," he said in a voice so soft that Ollie could hardly hear what he said. Thor moved aside and Erik stood by the vacated chair.

The giant leaned menacingly forward, towering over the frail German. Erik waited for a long time, his eyes glaring through the ski mask. Suddenly he bellowed, "You do not remember me. I was the Viking you offered a reward for if I was captured." He laughed so loudly that the prisoner tried to move back. "You do not remember me, Herr Gestapo chief? I almost captured you one night when the bombs exploded near your headquarters. Do you remember me now?" He stood to his full height, breathing hard.

Ollie wished that he could be the prosecutor. He wanted to suspend Kraus from the wall with chains on his wrists as the man had done to little Ake. He wanted to beat the former Gestapo commander as his soldiers had done to Valdy.

"I was the Viking you never caught," Erik continued. "I arranged the explosions so that we could rescue your prisoners, and we almost caught you. Remember? Do you remember me now?" Erik pulled off his mask, his red hair wild with static electricity. He leaned over, his face a foot from Kraus'.

Kraus remained silent, but Ollie could see that the muscles in his face and neck had tightened, and his hands and whole body now shook slightly. But Kraus remained silent, looking straight ahead, as if through Erik. Ollie hoped that Kraus would not have a heart attack and die before they were finished and could turn him over to the proper court for a real trial.

"You had better start talking before I grow angry, you stinking piece of shit," Erik roared in the prisoner's trembling face. "I can still break every rotten bone in your fucking body with my bare hands."

"I don't know you," Kraus finally mumbled. "I am an old man who is sick. I forget things." Kraus bowed his head, away from Erik's stare.

Once there was a time, Ollie thought, that Kraus would not have flinched. He had never looked away from Ollie while he was torturing him for all those hours.

"I am a sick old man," Kraus repeated. "I am the consul's father. I was not here before this year. May I have some water, please?" It sounded almost rehearsed, almost like a broken old record.

Ollie looked at Thor, who had moved next to Erik as though to prevent violence. "Yes, we will give you water," Thor replied. "That is more than you did for your prisoners, one of whom is here and would love to smash your face as you smashed his. But we will give you a drink."

Kraus looked around at the masked men as though he was trying to guess which of them had been his prisoner, and who might attack him.

Lars went in the next room and brought back a bottle of water. Kraus downed it in noisy gulps. Then he said, "I must go to the bathroom again. I must go often because I am old and sick."

"Certainly, Colonel Kraus," Thor replied in a kindly tone.

Kris turned off the tape recorder as Thor said, "G. you will take the Colonel to take a pee. And Herr Kraus, do not try to escape. It would be impossible, and the wolves probably would catch you if we did not. There are many hungry wolves on this mountain. In fact, we would enjoy seeing you eaten by wolves. But we really need to finish our conversation here. If you talk, we will turn you over to the authorities for a formal trial where you will be allowed to have a defense attorney. If you don't cooperate, we will try you here and now. So you better start talking soon. Remember, a member of our group knows too well what you did. He would like to do the same things to you. If you don't talk, I will let him work on you as you did to him."

Ollie watched Kraus and Gunnar leave for the bathroom. "He's a tough old bastard," he said, "but I don't think he's as feeble as he pretends to be. I've been watching his eyes and most of the time they are very alert. I think he is playing for time and hoping that he will be rescued."

"You're probably right, Ollie," Kris responded, "but time is on our side. We are younger and stronger than he is. We control the situation. As for rescue, this is a very safe place. No one comes here except in hunting season."

Thor told Ollie that Eduard had built the cabin many years before and his family came occasionally for a quiet weekend. He had built it so that he could escape from the same fish warehouse where Ollie's equipment had been stored briefly during the war.

The bathroom door opened and Gunnar and the prisoner returned. Gunnar roughly pushed the old man into his seat again, Kris turned on the tape recorder, and the interrogation continued. For three more hours Kraus insisted he was innocent, but he was tiring and The Fishermen knew it. He slumped slightly in his chair. His face grew gray. He sat, grimly staring at each of his captors, one by one. When he came to Ollie, he paused as if he had a glimmer of recognition. He almost seemed to smile, or so Ollie thought.

Turning to Thor, Ollie said, "I am the only one here who this bastard tortured. I think it's time for me to act as the prosecuting attorney. Does anyone object?"

Thorvald looked hard at Ollie's face, which Ollie felt heating up underneath the mask. "Remember your rules, O., he is innocent until proven guilty. "

"Shit, he is guilty," Erik growled. "Just let N. and me take him outside for a few minutes and he'll start talking."

"No, E., we agreed no violence," Ollie replied. "We will give the prisoner a chance to defend himself. You did not do that for your captives Colonel, did you?" he asked in a soft voice.

There was no answer.

"Herr Kraus do you remember the Gestapo building on Kong Oscarsgate?" Again there was no reply, the prisoner simply staring blankly into Ollie's eyes.

"Tell me about the basement room where you kept prisoners and made them talk," Ollie demanded as his voice became harder and more insistent. He felt the anger rising and his mind returned to those terrible days and the tortures he endured. "Herr Gestapo Colonel Kraus, answer me or I will let my large friends take you outside."

Kraus said, "I am a naval historian and I am the consul's father. You will go to jail for this. There are laws against kidnapping." His lips drew tight in a smirk.

"You tortured me," Ollie said sternly. "For six days you gave me only bread and water. You shocked me with an electric prod. You hung me by a chain from the wall. I was the American who worked with the underground and sent radio messages to the British. Now do you remember me, Herr Kraus?" He pulled off his mask as he said, "I remember you all too well."

Kraus smiled and stared calmly back at Ollie. "You were a spy. We should have shot you."

Suddenly the years of Ollie's nightmares came crashing back, memories he had finally been able to repress that now made him hurt all over as if he was Kraus' prisoner again. He remembered Kraus' cruelty. He thought of what later happened to Ake and Valdy and his anger grew. The bile rose in his stomach and into his throat and he had to swallow hard to keep from vomiting. His face turned bright red. He walked around the small table, grabbed the frail German by his shirt collar, and shook the man violently.

The room grew still. It was as if none of the former Fishermen was even breathing. "That's enough, O.," Ollie heard Thor say.

But Ollie couldn't stop.

"Talk, you bastard. Admit it. You were the Gestapo chief in Bergen during the war, yes? Talk or I'll kill you," Ollie roared in fury, forgetting the pledge he had made the other Fishermen take, losing his temper as he had not done since he was a small boy. He raised Kraus from his chair, the old man's body rigid as he tried to pull Ollie's hands from his neck.

"Ja," Kraus managed to say, "I was the Gestapo chief."

"Say it again," Ollie said as he stopped shaking the man, still holding on tightly to his collar. "Say it clearly so we have it all on tape."

"Ja, I was the Gestapo chief," Kraus said, gasping for breath as Ollie let go of him. He rubbed his neck with his hand and turned his head from side to side. Then he looked straight at Ollie and said, "I was only obeying orders from Himmler. And I made a mistake, ja? I was too nice. I should have killed you and the other collaborators on the spot. If only we had developed a bomb in time, we would have won." Then he spat in Ollie's face.

Erik pulled Ollie away before Ollie had a chance to grab Kraus again. Lars pushed Kraus into the chair and used a rope to tie his hands behind his back. Kris turned off the tape recorder.

"You have done more than what you had to, Olaf," Thor said, putting his hand on Ollie's shoulder, which was still heaving from effort. After a few moments, Ollie covered Thor's hand with his own.

chapter eight

THOR USED HIS cell phone to call his friend who was a prosecutor in the justice department and within an hour federal police arrived at the cabin to arrest Kraus for wartime crimes. "My friend believes that Norway will want to try Kraus," Thor said to Ollie in the car on the way to Erik's house. "He called Kraus the 'Monster.'"

"He was a monster back then," Ollie said, "and he still is now."

There were three messages at Erik's house for Ollie from Polly to call, no matter the hour. He dialed her and she answered quietly. "Tell me you're all right," she said.

"We just got back from fishing," he said.

"For the big fish?" she asked.

"Yes," he told her.

"What happened?" she asked.

"I'll tell you when I get home," he said. "It was a rough trip and I need to get some sleep now."

"But you're OK?" she asked.

"Yes," he told her. "I am."

"I'll see you in a day," she said.

"Yes," he said once again before he told her that he loved her.

He slept for a little more than four hours. When Ollie woke, Thor was in Erik's kitchen waiting for him. "Both Erik and Kris were called away to work. Kris has arranged for his pilot to take you to Kirkenes to see your friend. I'm to accompany you as your translator," Thor said.

They took Kris' small jet north on a flight that carried them over lush forests, glistening glaciers, and a quiet shoreline that once had been patrolled by the German navy, and where its war ships had hidden. Looking out the window Ollie could see the ocean and dozens of small islands as well as a scattering of fishing boats and one large ocean liner carrying tourists up the rocky coast. After landing at the airport, Ollie and Thor rented a car and headed to Kirkenes.

"Where to?" Thor asked.

"I'm not exactly sure," Ollie said. He pulled out his wallet and slipped Kirsten's letter from it. "I have an address but I don't know if it's current."

"It's a start," Thor said.

Once they reached the town, Thor stopped at a filling station and asked the attendant for directions to the address that Ollie provided. They ended up on a narrow street of small, wood-rotted houses with peeling paint. While sitting in the car before approaching the door of the house whose address matched the one on his letter, Thor said, "Who exactly are we looking for?"

"A friend," Ollie said. He paused and looked out the window at the over-grown yard. "She was more than a friend, actually."

Thor was quiet for a moment, then said, "If you don't mind me asking, who is she?"

Ollie took Kirsten's photograph from the envelope and told him about meeting her during his recuperation after his time in Bergen. "I had hoped to return to Bergen after the war so that we could get married, but I couldn't get back to Norway," Ollie said. "Just before the war ended I was wounded in a bombing raid on London and I spent many months in hospitals. Then when I got home my parents had grown old and sick, and there was no money for the trip. She wrote me one letter about a year after my return, in which she told me that she'd married a Norwegian soldier from Kirkenes. So slowly over the years I stopped thinking of Kirsten every day. Eventually I made a new life. But I've always wondered what happened to her."

"Let's go and find out," Thor said, handing the photo back to him.

Ollie knocked on the door but no one was home. He and Thor went next door and an older woman talked to Thor. Ollie watched her gesturing with her hands, pointing to the house and then to her head. Thor turned to Ollie and said that many years before Kirsten's husband had died and she had had a nervous breakdown. Now she lived in a rest home on the edge of town. Ollie thanked the woman for the information.

"I'm sorry to hear about your friend," Thor said.

"Well, now I know," Ollie told him, shaking his head.

"You've come this far. You should see her," he told him.

Ollie nodded. "I may never have another chance."

After stopping at a pay phone and looking up the nursing home in the phone book, Thor called the facility and asked for directions. He found the home easily. It was a simple and solidly built white-painted wooden house that had once belonged to a rich merchant. It had a long porch in front with a row of rocking chairs. From the street there was a pathway lined with bright red and yellow flowers and four steps leading up to the house. A woman in a white nurse's uniform met them at the door. Thor explained the reason for their visit. The woman went inside and found the manager.

Ollie showed her the photo. She studied it for a long time before saying in English, "We call her Kirsty. A beautiful young woman you will not see. But if you sit down in the lounge over there, I will bring her out to you. She has grown old, sir, and you may not recognize her. I did not realize how beautiful she had been. Or how lively she must have been. What a wonderful warm smile she had." She handed the photograph back to Ollie. "She may be emotional because she does not get many visitors anymore, just her son and her in-laws, but some months they don't bother to visit."

Then she left to find Kirsten.

"I'll wait for you in the car," Thor said.

"But you'll need to translate for me," Ollie told Thor. "We only ever spoke Norwegian back then. I'm sure she doesn't know English."

Thor took a deep breath. "Of course," he said. He patted Ollie on the shoulder as they walked into the lounge and sat down on a couch. Across from Ollie and Thor was a television that was on but no one was watching it. There were several very old people sitting in wheelchairs staring off into space. Two old ladies sat reading books near a window looking out on a garden. After about five minutes the manager wheeled an elderly lady beside Ollie. He looked at her carefully. This was Kirsten? Her face was lined and puffy. Her eyes were watery. She had lost most of her teeth and she didn't even look over at him, unaware that she had a visitor.

Ollie had to fight to control his emotions. Kirsten had become heavy and bent over, as though her back no longer could hold her straight. It was hard to recognize her, but he still could see the familiar eyes and the small mole on her cheek. His once beautiful girl was now an old woman obviously suffering from Alzheimer's disease.

"Go ahead," Thor said. "I'll tell her whatever you want."

"Kirsten, I am Ollie, remember?" Ollie finally asked, leaning close to her.

Thor translated but the woman didn't look at either man. There seemed to be no recognition of them or anything being said.

"We met during the war and we wanted to get married but I had to leave." His voice caught just as Thor started translating.

The woman sat hunched over, gazing at her hands.

"I lived in your father's barn," he said before Thor followed with the Norwegian translation.

Ollie touched her hand softly and said, "We had a baby, but he died."

Quietly, Thor spoke in Norwegian.

Kirsten lifted up her head to look at Ollie's face. He thought he saw a flicker of recognition. And then she started speaking in a hoarse whisper.

Thor told him, "She says you're not her husband. He was a drunk and beat her, then he ran away with another woman. She says she loved an American."

Ollie could hardly breathe. Yes, she had loved him as he had loved her, but her life had been tragic because he didn't return. The guilt made him want to run, and to turn the clock back, but that was impossible. So he continued to hold her hand while she watched the television—some program on train travel—until the manager returned to wheel Kirsten back to her room.

Tears sliding down his cheeks, Ollie kissed Kirsten gently on the forehead and left with Thor to return to Bergen.

...

The next day Erik, Thor, and Kris took Ollie to the airport. This time there were only a few people, all strangers, in the waiting area. The four former Fishermen stood quietly near the gate as passengers began to board the plane. The farewell was a stark contrast with the *Velkommen* scene only a few days earlier. It was as if everything had been said.

Finally Erik put his large arms around Ollie in a bear hug, making him gasp momentarily for breath. "Ollie," he said, "there are no words to tell you how much we have enjoyed our reunion with you. *Ja*, you came back as you said you would. We are very grateful."

Next it was Kris's turn to hug Ollie. His voice was choked with emotion and he said, "We could not have done this without you, and we appreciate your long trip to help us. We will never forget you."

Thor stood silently while his friends spoke. Finally he hugged Ollie. In a voice that was barely audible, he said, "We did not convict Kraus, but we did get the bastard. Now the chapter is closed. Ollie, we all can be proud. But also, on behalf of all your friends, it has been wonderful having you back for this short time."

As he began to reply Ollie saw tears in Thor's eyes, and he realized that his own eyes were filling, but he was not embarrassed. He had done his duty. He had returned to Bergen. And maybe now the war was over. "My friends, I will always remember this visit and all that you have done to make it good," he said. "As you know, there were a few sad moments, particularly when I saw Ake, Evold, and yesterday, Kirsten, but there also was much more that was happy, and I am so glad that I could see all of beautiful Bergen in daylight this time. And, of course, we captured the monster." He paused and took several deep breaths before continuing. "I am sad because I doubt that I ever will be able to return for another reunion." His voice cracked for a minute and then he said, "Thank you. *Takk so milka*. Now I will have more good memories of Norway and my friends, The Fishermen."

With that he turned and handed his ticket to the SAS agent at the gate and slowly walked down the jetway to the waiting airplane.

JONATHAN MARSHALL was born in 1924 and raised in New York City. He graduated from the Fieldston School. He received a bachelor's degree in political science and economics from the University of Colorado. He later took graduate courses at the University of North Carolina in city planning and worked as a planner for more than four years, leaving to work for Adlai Stevenson's presidential campaign.

In 1953 he purchased a bankrupt magazine, *The Art Digest*, which he later renamed *Arts*. After bringing the magazine into the black, he accepted a job with the Ford Foundation's Humanities and Arts Program.

But publishing was in his blood and he later left the Ford Foundation to pursue a master's degree in journalism at the University of Oregon in Eugene, Oregon, where he moved with his wife, Maxine, and two daughters. Once he graduated, Marshall naively decided to try to buy a small daily newspaper. After a year of searching he bought the bankrupt *Scottsdale Daily Progress* and moved his family, which also includes two sons, to Scottsdale, Arizona.

Marshall published the *Scottsdale Daily Progress* for 25 years and wrote more than 12,500 editorials and columns as well as articles for several journalism publications. He was inducted into the Arizona Newspaper Association's Hall of Fame and the University of Oregon's Communication Hall of Achievement. In addition, he was awarded the national Society of Professional Journalists' Sigma Delta Chi Foundation's First Amendment Award. Marshall was twice nominated for Pulitzer Prizes and twice was a Pulitzer juror. He sold the *Scottsdale Daily Progress* in 1987 and the Marshalls used the proceeds to start a charitable foundation.

In 1992, the Marshalls toured Scandinavia and visited a number of World War II landmarks, including a one-room museum in Bergen, Norway, which told the story of a local resistance group that had provided intelligence information by radio on German naval activity in the North Sea. The group's story intrigued Marshall and he conceived the idea of *Reunion in Norway*, based on the efforts of the Norwegian resistance. The underground war activities were vital in the Allied campaign against the Nazis but have received little attention outside of Norway.

Marshall lives in Paradise Valley, Arizona. In addition to their four children, he and his wife have seven grandsons.